To Pame
with

Jane

BEASTS & LOVERS

First published 2012 by Beggar Books
An imprint of Fast-Print Publishing of Peterborough, England

FastPrint
Publishing

www.fast-print.net/bookshop

Beasts & Lovers
Copyright © Jane Corbett 2012

ISBN: 978-178035-327-2

A catalogue record for this book is available from the British Library

An environmentally friendly book printed and bound in England by
www.printondemand-worldwide.com

Mixed Sources
Product group from well-managed
forests, and other controlled sources
www.fsc.org Cert no. TT-COC-002641
© 1996 Forest Stewardship Council
FSC

PEFC Certified
This product is
from sustainably
managed forests
and controlled
sources
www.pefc.org
PEFC
PEFC/16-33-415

This book is made entirely of chain-of-custody materials

Jane Corbett is a novelist and screenwriter, who taught in Further and Higher Education for many years, and currently is at the national Film and Television School.

Illustrations by Sean Victory
Email: sean_victory@hotmail.com

With special thanks to Julia Casterton, Barry Devlin,
Loveday Herridge, Kate Saunders, and Bettina Wilhelm
for their precious time and invaluable advice.

The Frog Prince

Exams were over. Nothing to do but eat, sleep and party for the foreseeable future. Instead of elation Kay felt a sense of anticlimax. All her life she had raced towards the next goal, for she was nothing if not ambitious. Now there was a vacant horizon. The strategies by which she had hitherto ordered her life had at a stroke become superfluous.

Her parents often remarked what a lovely girl she was and her girlfriends envied her her figure. Most of their talk was about looks and clothes and several of them suffered tortures of feeling not pretty or sexy enough. Kay didn't share their preoccupations. Stubbornly she was determined, for the time being at least, to remain within the safety zone of the non-contender. She had nothing against boys but had never had a boyfriend.

The disadvantage of this was that as her peers paired off and became more sexually active, she found herself at parties or on occasions which required twosomes, teamed up with the nerds and social no-hopers. At seventeen she was the only girl in her class to remain a virgin, which resulted in further loss of status. A few of the more adventurous young males were spurred on by her manifest sex appeal but soon lost interest in favour of more available targets.

As the odd one out she sometimes found herself thrown into the company of a boy called Francis Conroy, known by some as Froggy Francis because of his chubby, rather formless body and large moist hands. He was a serious boy, whose main aim like her own was to stay out of the firing line of aspiring alpha males. But, unlike Kay, he wasn't particularly good at schoolwork or on the sports field. In fact he did as little as possible to attract attention to himself, and could usually be found sitting on a bench at the end of a school corridor or in some corner of the playground reading or listening to his Iplayer. The one thing he enjoyed was swimming, which he pursued whatever the weather, though he avoided competitions and wasn't a member of a team. He was the last person to abandon the outdoor pool at the end of summer when the days grew colder and the first to return there as soon as the sun began to warm up in spring. He went about in baggy grey trousers and a dusty blazer, which failed to hide his rotund stomach and oddly muscular thighs. His hair fell over his large protuberant eyes that were the colour of pond water, partially obscuring his vision, but he refused to cut it. Despite such irritations, Kay found the undemanding nature of his presence preferable to the more pushy boys.

One Saturday afternoon she was seated in front of her dressing table brushing her long hair, which reached in a shining sheaf to her shoulder blades. The rhythmic strokes of the brush had a soothing, hypnotic effect. She was considering the empty days ahead and wondering if she should get a job or accept her parents' offer of a holiday in Spain, when her mother shouted up the stairs that she had a phone call. Reluctantly she laid down the brush and got up.

'Hallo?'

'Kay? It's Francis. I wondered if you were going to the party tonight.'

'What party?'

'The school leavers' party. Had you forgotten?'

She had deliberately put it out of her mind.

'They've gone to a lot of trouble. It seems a bit churlish not to go.'

He used words like 'churlish', another of his weird traits.

'I think we should support them.'

'What's with the "we"?'

'I mean the class.'

She said nothing.

'Kay?'

'Sorry. What time does it start?'

'Eight.'

'O.K. Maybe see you there around 9.30.'

She rang off before he could reply.

Many of the students would be bringing their boyfriends and girlfriends and she had no intention of being paired off with Froggy Francis. On the other hand it could be useful to have him there in case … in case of what she wasn't sure.

There were a couple of hours to kill before she needed to get ready so she went back to her room, picked up a pile of magazines from the floor and began flicking through them. After two years of A-level set texts, this was an indulgence she'd been looking forward to. But as the expected hit failed to register, she cast aside one after the other. At the bottom of the pile was a copy of one of her brother's soft porn mags. He must have left it in her room to escape detection from their parents. She stared at the scantily clad women and posturing men, striking attitudes to display their testosterone fuelled bodies. In one picture you could make out a tuft of pubic hair peeking over the guy's bulging thong. The image stirred the silt of memory like bubbles rising to the surface. Her father was coming out of the shower, towelling himself vigorously. The towel slipped to reveal his large, slightly erect penis and wrinkled scrotum, red as a turkey's neck. His stout body was covered with reddish gold fuzz and at the base of his belly was a triangle of pubic hair, whose fiery colour matched the hairs in his ears and on the backs of his hands. He grinned at her as he swept past. He reminded her of one of the satyrs in a book she had of illustrated Greek myths and she quickly checked his feet for cloven hooves. He was the first adult male she had ever seen in all his fleshly glory and for years the image continued to arouse the same mixture of excitement and revulsion that would not go away.

The school party had a 1950's theme and the gym had been transformed into a dancehall, complete with mirrored ball casting shafts of glittering colour, blue, red, and indigo, as it revolved above the dancers. Girls wore blouses tucked into belted skirts with ballet slippers on their feet and boys had greased their hair, John Travolta style, and wore shirts with bootlace ties and whatever footwear most resembled brothel creepers. Kay was seized upon by a group of girls and hustled over to the drinks table. A DJ was playing Elvis records and the floor was heaving with bodies.
    'You look great, Kay!'
    'A guy's been asking about you.'
    'Really. Who?'
    'Over there. Cute, eh?'

Kay searched the crowd for the boy in question, as her friend was swept onto the dance floor. One by one the girls peeled off but the promised suitor failed to materialise. There was no sign of Francis either, though she'd have been glad even of him in order to feel less conspicuous. She topped up her wine glass and felt a tap on her shoulder. She turned to find herself face to face with a boy she recognised as one of the elite scholarship group. She'd seen him around but didn't know his name. The music was so loud he had to bend down and shout in her ear.

'Fancy a dance?'

'I'm waiting for a friend.'

She tried to sound casual.

'You can dance while you wait.'

He smiled and held out his hand. The dance floor was a mass of furiously jigging bodies. The jive craze had hit the class after a visiting group of actors had held a drama workshop and taught them to dance. Girls were tossed in the air over their partner's shoulders and thrust dizzyingly down between their legs to resurface and resume their frenzied gyrations. To Kay the experience of being thrown around by a stranger in the hope of being caught wasn't pleasant and after a few moments she begged to leave the floor.

'I need some fresh air.'

It was true; the temperature in the gym had reached boiling point. He led her round the edge of the dance floor to the doors at the back, which opened onto the playground. Outside he produced a packet of cigarettes, took two and lit them, holding one out for Kay. She took it, though she didn't really smoke, and after a couple of puffs discreetly let it drop to her feet.

'I've noticed you around. That guy you hang out with, Francis. Is he your boyfriend?'

'No way!'

'I thought not. You're much too gorgeous.'

There was a pause. She searched around for something to say.

'Got any plans for the summer?'

'I'm going to Canada. White-water rafting with my brother.'

'Is that dangerous?'

'Not if you don't mind getting drenched. There are a lot of rapids.'

She had no taste for extreme sports and the thought of getting half drowned in rapids held scant appeal. Her mind went back to cycling trips they'd taken as a family, to places like Brittany and the west coast of France. That was before her grandparents died and her mother inherited their house and there was money for proper holidays. Cycling meant keeping an eye on the road, with no time to take in the scenery, and such an expense of effort that once supper was eaten all one could do was fall into bed.

She stood with her back against the wall, as he took a step closer and placed his hands on the bricks at either side of her head. His face was very close and she could smell the alcohol mingled with cigarette smoke on his breath. It wasn't unpleasant. His face came closer until it was a blur. She shut her eyes, waiting for his kiss. His mouth closed on hers, his tongue insinuating itself between her lips to explore the moist cave of her mouth. She felt as if she were weightless, a specimen pinned to the wall by gravity, like on the Wall of Death.

'You're so sexy!' he breathed between kisses.

The muscles of his abdomen felt hard and firm and between the thighs pressing against hers, she felt his penis thrust itself with blind insistence into her groin. She pushed him away and almost ran back into the gym. As she squeezed through the dancers she saw Francis standing next to the DJ, attempting to engage him in conversation.

'About bloody time! I thought we agreed 9.30.'

Her fury took him by surprise.

'I didn't think you'd be waiting. You just said you might come.'

'Same thing, stupid!'

The DJ put on a slow song by some woman singer.

'Want to dance?'

'I'm going home.'

She turned and walked rapidly away.

That night she dreamed of a huge slimy frog. It entered her room and tried to climb into her bed, but she carried it to the window and threw it out in disgust. A hot wave of pleasure ran through her as the ugly thing fell splat onto the path below.

Some of the class had agreed to catalogue the local fauna and flora for a nature conservancy organisation. It was the final event before leaving school. To his surprise, Kay asked Francis to be her partner. She'd been absent on the day most people paired up, largely to avoid any complications with the boy from the dance. It was a pretty safe bet that Francis would have remained unpartnered.

It was hot and humid as, armed with a notebook and camera, they wandered through the fields and the half-uprooted remains of hedgerows. For two days they came across little of interest and eventually gave up and repaired to Kay's garden. It was a large garden surrounded by a wall, collapsed in places so that rabbits and muntjacs from the neighbouring woods came in to feed. Its untended wildness gave shelter to a host of plants, birds and small mammals, far more varied than the over-cultivated farmland.

The heat, which continued to rise, made her relaxed and lethargic. Everything had slowed down, and with no more obligations the days were once again left to chance. They lay on their backs in the long grass of the unkempt lawn, gazing up at the sky with its scarcely moving clouds. Her parents were at work and there was nothing to break the silence but the lazy drone of insects and the occasional plane passing across the distant sky. Kay felt the pulses beating in the hollow of her throat and the crooks of her knees and elbows. Her limbs rested heavy and solid against the earth and her mind drifted in limbo. A shiver passed through her, making her nipples harden, but she did not register this nor the moistness between her thighs as the stirrings of desire. Eyes closed, cheeks flushed by sun and her own daring, she reached out a hand toward Francis.

He lay so still he might have been unconscious. Light as a moth, her fingers traced the contours of his belly and the roundness of his thighs, and still he did not move. Emboldened, she continued her exploration. With a will of its own her marauding hand slipped beneath the elasticated waistband of his tracksuit, moving down until it reached the heat of his erection. The nest of coarse hair from which it rose would not, she thought, be satyr-red but muddy brown like pond water.

The subjugation of this body to her touch excited her beyond measure with a sense of her own power. She could do with him what she would, kill him if she so desired. Unable to restrain himself any longer, Francis emitted a groan of pleasure and ejaculated into her hand. She snatched it back, wiping it furiously on the grass and sat up.

Despite her initial disgust, that afternoon became the first of many such explorations, taking place in secrecy and sometimes darkness so that even their own eyes were not witness to their abandonment. In the freedom of anonymity, and with no word spoken, the things she would have found intolerable in the light of day, the squashy pliancy of his willing body and the devotion of his liquid gaze, thrilled her.

Then, one day, as suddenly as the obsession had begun, it was over. She made the decision to yield to pressure and accompany her parents on holiday to Spain. She announced to Francis she was leaving the following week, after which she would be taking a holiday job at her uncle's hotel in St Ives. Francis, devastated, begged that at least they might write to each other but she refused. A clean break would be best for both of them, she declared, especially since they'd be going to different universities in the autumn.

The summer in St Ives was hard work, long days with early starts and late finishes, but Kay thrived. The weather was mostly fine and she was aware, for the first time in her life, that she was happy. She loved swimming in the sea on her afternoons off and hired a wet suit. There were a couple of nice girls working at the hotel and in their free time the three of them went down into the local town and met up with some other young people, mostly from Europe doing holiday jobs. She went out a few times with a German boy but stopped short of full sex, partly because of his obsession with sexually transmitted diseases. The other girls assumed she had a proper boyfriend at home, some good-looking Lothario who knew how to fuck. She smiled and said she had in the past but now it was over. She intended to keep herself free from entanglements, waiting for her real life to begin.

One day she received a letter from Francis, sent from Ibiza and forwarded by her parents. He stopped short of any declaration but the tone of longing was unmistakable. She threw the letter into the waste paper basket, not wanting the warm feelings that remained to turn to revulsion. Whatever had existed between them, it had happened to another person in another life.

At the end of the summer she returned home in time to get ready for university. She would be spending the first term in hall and, after that, hoping to find a flat. On the final night before her departure, she invited a few friends over for a farewell get-together. At ten o'clock there was a ring on the doorbell. She went downstairs and opened the door. A young man stood there. He was of medium height with a head of silky dark hair and eyes the colour of pond water. She stared at him for a moment, as her stomach clenched in recognition.

'Are you going to ask me in?'

The smile he gave was charming.

'Francis? My God! You've changed!'

He had not so much slimmed down as straightened out, as if someone had stretched him on the rack and in the process flattened out the roundness of shoulders and stomach. His previous, slightly flabby pallor had transformed into a muscular tan and that, together with his new haircut, took away the froggy nature of his appearance. It must have been all the swimming in Ibiza or perhaps he'd been working out at a gym. Whatever it was, the frog had turned, if not into a prince, at least into a presentable looking young man.

'I hope for the better.'

Kay did not reply. She was taking in the confident stranger in front of her. He had an air of expectancy, as if waiting to claim her as due reward for his transformation. Every instinct rose up within her in furious resistance.

'I'm off to uni in the morning,' she said briskly.

'Tomorrow?'

He couldn't hide his disappointment.

'Maybe I could drive you? I passed my test.'

'Thanks, but my parents are taking me. You know how important things like leaving home are to them.'

'Will I see you before you go?'

'No time, I'm afraid. But join us for a drink, if you like. You know everyone here.'

It took a moment for him to take in the destruction of his hopes. Then he bid her a polite goodnight and she watched him as he walked away down the street, without looking back.

Albatross

A young reporter, on his first assignment for his local paper, entered the taproom of the Cock and Feathers. The pub was just off the high street, a vestige of a small market town swallowed up in the creeping expansion of south London. He himself had been brought up in the area, his parents having bought a house on a newly built estate soon after he was born.

He'd chosen to write a piece on 'Our Changing Neighbourhood' and the Cock and Feathers had a reputation for 'characters', with stories to tell and memories that went back a long way. One such was Dave Minter, likened by some to the Ancient Mariner because he was apt to buttonhole any passing stranger to regale them with his tale.

It was just before the lunchtime rush and the place was still quiet. The reporter went up to the bar and placed his tape recorder on the counter.

'Hi, I'm Francis,' he said to the publican. 'You agreed to give me a few minutes.'

'Oh, yes! The young man from the paper. So what exactly did you want to know?'

'I'm doing a piece about the neighbourhood. This is one of the oldest pubs, a real local like you don't often find these days. I'd like you tell me a bit about it, your regulars, that sort of thing.'

'O.K. Fire away.'

Francis spoke softly into his mic.

'September 5th, 2008, interview with John Higgins, landlord of 'The Cock and Feathers'... John, tell me about your oldest customer. I've heard he's quite a character.'

He nodded at the publican to start speaking.

'You're referring to old Dave? He's lived round here for more than seventy years. His house, like everything else in these parts, is under threat from developers. They say it'll either be torn down or turned into offices. I tell you, it won't be long before they get their hands on this place!'

Francis attempted to steer the man back to his question.

'So what about Dave?'

'Poor old boy! He's got no one so he'll probably be sent to an old people's home. He's in here every day, lunchtimes and sometimes again in the evening. The other day a woman from Social Services comes looking for him. She claims he's refusing to respond to their letters and calls and they're concerned for his safety. He knows they're trying to get him out of his place and swears he'll only leave when they carry him out, feet first. He's a fighter, I'll say that for him! Basically, like most of the regulars, he's lonely and just wants to talk.'

'What sort of thing does he talk about?'

The publican chuckled.

'You'd be surprised! He's got this theory about a fourth dimension, as he calls it. Most of us, apparently, believe in three. But there's some guy called Blackwell who claims to have discovered a fourth. According to Dave his theory's backed up by writings from the past, all of which testify to some ancient knowledge man's long forgotten. Something like Stonehenge measuring the movement of the planets before anyone had telescopes or compasses. Anyway, given half a chance Dave will tell you about a boy who flew a glider so far and so high, he broke right through into this fourth dimension and was never seen again. That's right, no body, no wreckage, nothing! Dave sees it as proof that time and space exist differently there, in some sort of parallel universe. The boy, he says, is still out there in a world we can only imagine. Unless, of course, you were also to break through... Oh, he's a character all right!'

*   *   *

Dave Minter wasn't a war hero. A teenage bout of TB had rendered him unfit for active service and he'd been forced to remain behind his desk in Whitehall, keeping the war machine running at home. In 1942 he married a young woman who worked in a munitions factory and a year later she bore him a son. They called him Ian. When the war ended and the fighting men came home, money was tight and jobs hard to find so Dave stayed on at the Ministry. His wife trained as a teacher so she could be at home for Ian when school finished and during the holidays.

In February 1953 Ian's class visited the Imperial War Museum. When he came home he started questioning his father about the destruction of Dresden and Berlin and the dropping of atom bombs on Hiroshima and Nagasaki. Dave, for whom nothing could dent his belief in a just war nor undermine his reverence for the glory of combat, did his best to answer his son's questions but without success. His father's war stories only increased Ian's feelings of unease and he experienced the first faltering of his child's faith in the universal rightness of adults. Equally hollow seemed his father's accounts of England single-handedly triumphant against the enemy, if you discounted the unforgivably late entry of the Americans to the war. He looked around him and all he saw were bombsites, shored-up buildings and exhausted, joyless people.

Then came the coronation and in defiance of the rain and grey skies, London exploded in an orgy of rejoicing and street parties. Ian and his parents were invited to a neighbour's house to watch the spectacle live on their nine-inch black-and-white TV, bought specially for the occasion. Everyone, including Ian, was given a glass of pink champagne to toast Her Youthful Majesty. But pretty soon life returned to normal.

Like several of his neighbours, Dave had constructed a shed in the back garden out of stuff he'd picked up here and there. He spent his evenings hammering and tinkering, whilst inside the house his wife sat marking schoolbooks or ironing and listening to the radio. Ian usually stayed in the kitchen with his mother until bedtime, especially in winter when it was dark and cold and the rest of the house was unheated. He was happy to share her silence, doing his homework or playing with his meccano set, cocooned in the warmth of his mother's presence. It was the only time he felt sure of her. His father dominated any room he happened to be in. But Ian often had the impression that once out of sight, his mother evaporated into thin air. For this reason he developed the habit of monitoring the least sign of turbulence or change of mood beneath her outer calm. It was an attempt to combat his fear of any small disruption that might destroy the precarious equilibrium of their lives.

Dave had a passion for planes and battleships and made models of them accurate to the last detail. For Ian's ninth birthday he constructed a replica of the battleship Vanguard, powered by batteries with remote control steering. They took it to sail on the pond in the park, where he was the envy of the boys from the neighbouring estate. One day he went to the pond by himself and a gang of them mobbed him and seized the boat. After they'd each had a turn and worn down the batteries, they smashed it to pieces and set fire to the remains. His father chided him for being a coward and not standing up for himself. But when his mother, in a rare burst of anger, shouted at his father to leave the boy alone, he felt more ashamed than ever.

At the age of thirteen, at his father's insistence, Ian was put in for the scholarship exam for Wellington, a boarding school chosen for its military connections. His mother's health was increasingly poor and she was given a term's leave of absence from the primary school where she taught a class of mixed ability. Despite her condition she managed to coach Ian in English and Maths for the exam, whilst his father took him through a series of daily verbal reasoning tests. His teachers had advised against his sitting the exam, saying it was foolish to raise the boy's hopes when he'd be up against prep school kids with all their assets of privilege and class. But to everyone's surprise he passed the exam, and one brisk September morning said goodbye to his mother, who had spent the last two weeks packing and unpacking his trunk, which was to follow by Carter

Patterson, and accompanied by his father took the train to Wellington.

The shock of institutional life was even greater than the shock of the other boys. It felt as though he was being ordered about and shouted at every minute of every day. Even at night he got no peace, surrounded by the snorting, muttering, farting boys in his dormitory where there was no space he could call his own. His half of the washstand between his own and his neighbour's narrow beds, was always covered with smears of alien toothpaste, stinky socks, snotty handkerchiefs and other sordid detritus not his own. He thought longingly of his cold bedroom with its books, drawings and half built meccano models. But when his thoughts turned to his mother, they stopped short. The aching anxiety inside him was like a cancer spreading in the dark and the only possibility was to bury it deep within. In comparison with that, the teasing and bullying of the other boys barely touched him, and the indifference he showed even to physical pain, quickly won him a reputation for toughness. When he was sent to Coventry he felt nothing other than mild relief and he was scarcely more affected by being made the butt of their frequent practical jokes, like an apple pie bed or his shoelaces tied together. The result was that his tormentors pretty soon left him alone, although they still called him a freak and a filthy pleb from a council estate. It was the first time he'd been made aware of his social class or the contempt one stratum felt for another. Occasionally, when the teasing got too much, he exploded in an outburst of uncontrolled rage, which further enhanced his reputation as a loner to be treated with a modicum of respect.

His first beating, administered by a prefect, was particularly shocking because it was received at the hands of a fellow pupil. Worse than the pain was the humiliation. It wasn't just a question of pupils versus staff, he realised, but a far more vicious hierarchy, based on those boys perceived to be officer material being seduced with privileges in order to exploit the rest. Mercifully the boy he had to fag for was too idle to be much of a bully and he accepted the duties imposed on him like he accepted having to wait at table because he was a junior. But at some point he began to realise that power was not simply a question of seniority, and that those not prepared to play the game would remain victims forever.

He himself had no interest in exercising authority over others and knew he would never be made a prefect. He developed an ability to make himself invisible in a room full of people and to slip away unnoticed, discovering the freedom of anonymity that allowed him to do more or less as he liked. At the same time he was also acquiring a taste for learning, in particular French literature and history. The history teacher was one of the few inspirational teachers in the school and cultivated a coterie of bright pupils, to which Ian yearned to be admitted. He specialised in the medieval period, which he brought vividly to life through his descriptions of its heresies and bloody religious wars.

Ian was excited by the big ideas they discussed in class, such as gnosticism with its belief in separate forces of good and evil. Despite his father's professed agnosticism he had never envisaged any alternative to Christianity, especially not one that did away at a stroke with the knotty problem of how a good, all powerful God allowed people to suffer needlessly, through no fault of their own, in the way his mother did.

At the spiritual heart of the school was not so much religion as the corps. Whilst Ian despised all the stuff about leadership and patriotic duty, he found unexpected pleasure in the outdoor activities that were a necessary part of it, such as hurling himself over obstacle courses, trekking over muddy hills and camping out under the stars. He'd always enjoyed physical exertion and away from the institution that held them all in thrall, the camaraderie between the boys was different, more spontaneous and genuine. The history set regarded such mindless activity with contempt and there was no doubt it created a barrier against his full acceptance. But as he progressed to the sixth form and his French group were reading Camus, Sartre and Baudelaire, being a loner began to take on a certain cachet. One of the boys from his class, with whom he'd shared a tent on a couple of school camping trips, invited him to stay during the summer at their family chateau near Bordeaux. He refused on the excuse that his mother wasn't well, conscious that being identified as the social upstart he was would only lead to embarrassment.

After his exams he returned home for the summer holidays and his father began talking about Sandhurst. He replied that he'd seen enough of that sort of thing in the school corps and wanted nothing whatever to do with the military. His father asked curtly what he proposed to do instead and he told him he wished to try for Oxbridge. It was a spontaneous answer but a sufficiently prestigious goal to stall his father for the time being. It also had the advantage of putting off national service, which was on the point of being abolished anyway. Something the nation would soon regret, his father retorted, and went on to demand how, without contacts or financial backup, Oxbridge would lead to any career other than teaching. Surely he'd seen enough of that life from his mother. She stayed out of the argument. Each day she was more distracted than ever. He noticed her waxy pallor and the skin grown slack around her jaw, and his heart clenched in fear. He couldn't bear the thought of her growing old or any further weakening of her fragile hold on life. Yet his father appeared to notice nothing and still she went to work, cooked their meals and did the laundry and the housework. Occasionally his father washed up after supper but only if she felt really bad. Lately Ian had begun to cook when she didn't feel up to it, simple things, but he enjoyed it. If it had been just himself and his mother, they could have cooked together but he sensed his father's disapproval.

In the summer he was going to France for an exchange visit via his school French group. There was no opportunity to talk with his mother alone before he left. Either she was exhausted after school or his father was there. She seemed almost to be avoiding him, she who had always been eager to share his every thought. When he tried to talk about his life at school, he had the impression she wasn't really listening and he grew angry and impatient. In revenge he began treating her with the same casual indifference he did his father, even though he hated himself for it.

When he came back from France he got a job working in a holiday camp on the south coast, returning home a couple of days before the beginning of the new term. It was his second year of A-levels and as the nights drew in and with the decision of his future still unresolved, something occurred which changed everything irrevocably. His mother took her own life. His father found her on his return from work, lying on her bed fully clothed having taken an overdose of the sleeping pills she'd secretly hoarded. He called an ambulance, which took her to hospital but she was pronounced dead on arrival. Ian was given a twenty-four hour exeat for the funeral. He didn't want to stay longer.

His mind went into slow motion and his body too felt sluggish, as if drugged. Everything appeared to be happening at a distance, and each action or decision took an age to complete. The funeral was a low key crematorium affair, though the chapel was full, mainly with his mother's colleagues and the parents of her pupils. Ian had asked his father if there could be a grave, somewhere to visit and lay flowers, but his father told him plots were hard to come by these days and in any case the church had a problem with suicides. After the ceremony they went to a hotel for tea and cakes, which his mother's colleagues had organised. Then Ian returned to school. He passed the journey in the buffet car and got drunk on beer, so that when he reached school he was sent straight to his dormitory. No further punishment was administered in view of his bereavement.

He remained at school for the rest of the year to take his A-levels then went home to be with his father. No more was said about Oxbridge, which would have required returning to school for a further term. His father assumed that after a period of mourning, he'd see sense, do his national service then think about a suitable career.

The house felt terrifyingly cold and strange, for which he was almost grateful. He couldn't have borne it if everything had been the same, except that she wasn't there. She had always been a pervasive presence, like sunlight or fresh air, something you recognise even whilst taking it for granted. Whilst his father was at work he spent the days wandering round the house, trying to recall as much as he could about the past when she was alive. He realised that it was always he who had done the talking, without considering what she might be feeling. He was overwhelmed by the sense of time lost through his own selfish egotism, and dreaded that he would never know why she'd done what she did and would have to live with the uncertainty for the rest of his days. He asked himself again and again whether she'd been capable at the time of realising how her action would destroy not only herself but all three of them. Or was her despair such that even that knowledge was no match against her compulsion to be erased from this earth?

After a couple of weeks, unable to bear the silence and the mouse wheel of his own thoughts, he got a job at the local hardware store. From childhood he had loved the smells of turpentine, creosote and new rope associated with such places. The physical labour of the job was more satisfying to him than serving customers. Each morning he put out bags of fertiliser, garden furniture, rakes, spades and watering cans in front of the shop and took them in again at evening. He spent his days fetching ladders, boxes of nails and coils of wire from the cellar, or mixing paint and measuring up for a garden shed. After supper, which Ian cooked, his father repeated his custom of retreating to his own shed. Ian took on most of the domestic work and, though his father was clearly grateful, he was too proud to say so. They spoke little and almost never about his mother but he saw how his father's firm belief in the order of things had been shattered. He had never had friends or been a man for the pub and despite the apparent incompatibility of his parents, Ian was aware for the first time of their mutual dependence. Once, his father came into the house earlier than expected for supper and saw Ian wearing his mother's apron. He let out a half-suppressed cry and disappeared for the next couple of hours. When finally he returned, nothing was said by either of them. But that night, instead of going back to his shed, he sat in a chair and read the paper, whilst Ian got on with the washing up.

For several months following his mother's death, Ian's mind seemed to have gone to sleep, whilst his body kept going in the mechanical repetition of daily tasks. He read nothing except an occasional glance at the newspaper. His father seemed quietly grateful for his presence and let the question of his future lie. At Christmas he planted some bulbs in pots and put them on the kitchen windowsill as his mother used to do. He found himself incorporating several of her habits into his daily routine, as if in that way he could keep something of her alive. He was aware these rituals pained his father but that couldn't be helped. Erasing all memory of her, as if she had never been, was no solution to their grief.

He took to travelling out of the city on Sundays, just to get away from the house and his father's gloomy presence. Since he had nowhere particular to go, he took the Greenline bus and rode out beyond the suburbs to the end of the line. Once there, he got out and walked around until it was time to take the bus back again. He found a release in the feeling of movement and the breeze on his face.

The following Sunday he made sandwiches to take with him and a flask of tea. When he reached the terminus, he walked down the lane and across a couple of fields until he came to a pub, where he sat down on a bench in the bright spring sunshine and ate his lunch. It was quite chilly and the other customers were inside. He was joined by a friendly robin who ate some of the cheese from his sandwich, and that night, for the first time in weeks, he fell asleep almost as soon as his head touched the pillow.

His Sunday excursions became a habit he looked forward to. One Sunday he fell asleep on the way home and the bus driver, who'd come to recognise him, woke him up when it came to his stop. After that, when the bus was relatively empty, they got into conversation. The driver asked him if he had a reason for his weekly journey and he said it was just to get into the country for some peace and fresh air. The driver said if that was what he was after, had he ever thought of taking up gliding. There was an old airfield a couple of miles from the terminus, used now by small private aircraft and a gliding club. He himself had been a gunner in the RAF and had a passion for aircraft, though after the noise and racket of fighter planes he preferred the silence of gliders. It was impossible, he said, to describe the thrill of these great silent birds and what it felt like to be riding the thermals in the empty sky, with only the rush of wind in your ears. Ian asked if anyone could join or whether you had to have previous training. The bus driver replied that teaching people how to fly was what the club was all about. Of course you had to pay.

All week as Ian fetched and carried in the hardware store, his thoughts kept returning to the description of gliding. He decided to ask the bus driver on the following Sunday if he would take him along to the airfield. But when Sunday came there was a different driver because it was the other man's day off. Ian got off the bus at the terminus and strolled around. But for the first time he felt restless, and instead of going for his usual walk caught the next bus back to town.

On the Monday after work, he went to the library and took out all the books he could find on the subject of gliders. He kept them in his room, in case his father saw them lying around and asked questions. Each evening, after he'd washed up the supper things and put them away, he went upstairs and pored over the books. When Sunday came, he asked the driver whether his offer to take him to the airfield still stood and they agreed to meet on his next Sunday off in two week's time. The driver would meet him at the terminus and take him there in his van.

Ian's excitement over the intervening weeks gave all the signs of his having fallen in love, and his father asked jokingly when he was going to meet the girl. He replied dismissively that he'd no time for girls but said no more. Up in his room he ransacked his wardrobe, trying to decide what to wear in case he got the opportunity to go up in one of the gliders. In the end he put on his usual jeans and windcheater and packed his school scarf and lucky cricket cap into his rucksack. He took money from his savings box under his bed, enough for a down payment on a course of tuition. He would make up the rest from his wages.

The bus arrived late at the terminus and the driver was already waiting. Ian scarcely recognised him without his uniform. He was dressed in casual cords and an old sheepskin flying jacket. At the entrance to the airfield, he showed his pass to the guard at the barrier and after a brief chat they were let through. They set off down a tarmac road, which cut through the flat grassland, until they reached a group of hangars sheltering beside a clump of tall pine trees. A row of light planes of varying shapes and sizes was drawn up alongside the sheds, some sleek and modern, others that had seen several years of service. Ian asked impatiently where the gliders were. The driver ribbed him for his eagerness and led the way to the last hangar. As he pulled open the heavy double doors, Ian saw six gliders lined up like giant white seabirds.

It was love at first sight. Not even the pictures he had studied endlessly had prepared him for their bird-boned elegance and impressive wing span. He turned to the driver.

'Any chance of a ride?'

Half an hour later he climbed into the narrow cockpit and took his seat in front of an instructor, hardly able to contain his excitement.

The sound of rushing air filled his head, as they skimmed along the concrete in the wake of the towing plane. It felt to Ian as if all his life had been leading up to this moment, and in the instant of lift off, as gentle as a kite taking to the air, he felt his heart lifting too. A faint buzz came from the engine of the other plane but apart from that there was only wind and silence, as behind him the pilot pulled the lever to release the tow rope. Ian watched it snake away into thin air and felt a frisson of terror as he realised they were now held aloft solely by their own momentum. The altimeter in the instrument panel in front of him said 2500 feet. Above them the sun shone brightly and, looking down, he saw the shadow of a great bird passing silently over a patchwork of fields below. It took a moment to recognise it as their own, as if for a brief fragment of time, this slender craft were some minute planet that eclipsed the sun.

For several days after his flight, the sense of euphoria remained. He said nothing to his father. Sometimes when he was younger he had tried to share some interest with him, out of a sense of filial duty. But experience had taught him otherwise. His father would bombard him with questions, demanding to have whatever it was described in such detail that all pleasure was sucked dry.

The following Sunday he got off the bus and walked to the airfield, where he made arrangements for a course of weekly gliding lessons. Sundays thus became the focus of his week. His father was pleased by the change in his son but also concerned that if something good had entered his life, he refused to talk about it. It perturbed him deeply that the boy seemed to have lost all ambition and was content to earn a bare living doing a menial job with no prospects. Was it for this they had sacrificed their own pleasures to give him the advantage of a good education? Yet he rarely went out in the evenings or got drunk like many young men, and he seemed to have no more of a social life than before.

One Sunday, unable to bear the suspense any longer, while his son was absent he went up to his bedroom. The door was locked but he kept a separate set of all the house keys and let himself in. It was not an action he performed lightly. Despite, or probably because of his irrepressible curiosity, Dave prided himself on his ability to respect another's privacy. He had always done his best to be aware of his faults and to counteract them wherever possible. He was prepared to admit he might sometimes have been too hard on Ian, in an attempt to make him stand on his own two feet and be less of a mother's boy. He had believed that was a father's duty, especially with an over indulgent mother and a father who wasn't a war hero. His own father had died when Dave was two so he had a rather theoretical notion of fathering. But now, as he gazed around at the walls covered with pictures of gliders, some torn out of magazines, some photographs Ian had most likely taken himself, he felt a deep sense of pride. All his suspicions were for naught. The boy had simply fallen in love with flying and in his wildest dreams he couldn't have wished for anything better. He took a closer look at one of the photographs, in which Ian sat smiling in the cockpit of a glider. He was wearing a leather flying jacket with a fur collar such as pilots wore in the Second World War. Dave had never seen him in it and wondered where he'd got it.

He turned to the bed, which, like the floor, was strewn with flying manuals and model planes in the process of being assembled or painted. He went over to the desk and flicked through the papers scattered there. There was an invoice for £50 for a course of gliding lessons at the Penshurst Flying Club. He replaced it carefully, fearful of discovery. It must have taken the lad an age to save up that much, after he'd paid for his keep. He felt a new respect for his son and suddenly an idea struck him. He could make up for all the harshness and miscommunication of the past by building him a glider of his own, the finest one possible. The gift would say to his son all the things that words could not.

Ian soon graduated to flying solo and was fast becoming a competent glider. He learned how to ride the thermals, to bank tightly then swoop down so that his wings seemed almost to skim the ground. His instructor was impressed by his pupil's daring, but sometimes he found it necessary to chide him for it. The first duty of a good pilot, he told him, was never to take needless risks. Aerobatics were a series of manoeuvres carried out with scientific precision, not an outburst of joie de vivre. But that was exactly what flying was for Ian, being able to wheel and soar through the air without the sound and stench of engines, or roll playfully along the contours of a hillside then pirouette and plummet earthwards like a buzzard spotting his prey. At such moments the plane and he became a single entity, its wings his wings, his only controls a stick and two rubber pedals. On occasions when he came close to disaster, barely managing to pull up over a hill as it sped towards him or skim the treetops, the adrenalin rush merely heightened a glorious sense of being alive that flying gave him. If it came to it, that was how he would choose to die.

Dave said nothing to Ian about his discovery and the fact that he spent even longer than usual in his shed went virtually unnoticed. He found a technical library in Westminster, not far from the COI building in Whitehall where he worked, which had the books he needed if he was to choose the most up to date kit for the most modern, aerodynamic design. Coincidentally, the librarian turned out to be a plane enthusiast himself and knew all about gliders. He was only too keen to advise and warned that when it came to actual construction, this could not be done at home or in his shed. Dave decided to approach Phil, the mechanic who for years had maintained his old Hillman and kept it running when most would have pronounced it a write-off. Phil had a workshop under one of the railway arches near where they lived. He pointed out that an engineless plane wasn't something he had any experience of as yet, but considered it an interesting challenge.

Dave was determined to keep the enterprise secret from Ian. He planned to tell him only when the glider was ready and they could take it to the airfield for a test flight. His one fear was that his son's anger at what he might see as spying on his private life would make him reject his gift. It wouldn't be the first time his enthusiasm had proved disastrous. He remembered more than one occasion when his wife declared furiously that his meddling had killed the boy's interest, though all he'd ever wanted was to encourage him. Perhaps if he'd kept him at home instead of sending him to boarding school and taken him into his confidence more, they'd be building the glider together. But it was too late now.

Ian's nineteenth birthday was approaching and Dave planned to have the glider ready by then. He had contacted the Flying Club and sworn them to secrecy. Phil and he were to transport it there in Phil's trailer on Saturday so that it would be waiting for him on Sunday.

The day dawned bright and a brisk April breeze blew the clouds away by early morning. The sun came out, bringing the land to life, and Dave could hardly contain his excitement. He'd enquired earlier what Ian was doing for his birthday and when he'd replied with uncharacteristic candour that he was going to a flying club, Dave had asked if he could accompany him. To his surprise Ian had agreed and they'd arranged that Dave would watch him fly then take him off for a pub lunch.

They walked the couple of miles from the bus stop to the airfield, talking little. The silence out there was less oppressive than in the confinement of a room and Dave was so preoccupied by the thought of presenting his son with the glider that he scarcely noticed anyway. The guard at the entrance to the airfield greeted Ian familiarly. They passed through the barrier and walked on in the direction of the hangars. As they approached, the mechanic came out of his hut and announced with a broad smile that everything was ready. His excited manner and the way in which he made reference to Dave alerted Ian. He watched the two of them chatting as they went ahead towards the hangar and suddenly he felt he was walking into a trap. If his father had been spying on him, what did all his speeches about respecting one another's privacy amount to? He should have suspected something when he'd asked to accompany him but he'd been prepared to give him the benefit of the doubt. He should have run and kept on running.

The mechanic reached the doors of the hanger. He pulled them open and stood aside. Ian stopped in his tracks, all previous thoughts erased. He was staring at the loveliest glider he had ever seen. He walked over to it and ran his hand over its smooth flanks. It was of a white so pure it seemed to emit light. In the little cockpit he could see the pale leather seats, blending perfectly with the feminine delicacy of the craft. She was not big as gliders went but he could see, just by looking at her, how finely balanced she was in proportions of wing to body and how light and manoeuvrable she would be.

'I made it for you,' he heard his father say.

His throat was too dry to answer. His father's face was filled with a mixture of pride and uncertainty. Ian found his voice.

'She's wonderful! Can I take her out?'

'She's yours. You can do whatever you want with her.'

He climbed into the cockpit to inspect the instrument panel and controls. Everything smelt new. He could scarcely take in that this perfect little craft was all his own. His father's eyes never left him as the mechanic continued to point out the small adjustments he'd made. Eventually Ian climbed down and together they moved the glider out to the launch area.

'Your father's done a terrific job,' the mechanic said as they hooked her up to the towing plane. 'She'll take you to 5000 feet and more. Easy! But remember, it's your first flight.'

Dave produced a bottle of champagne and three glasses from his rucksack to toast her maiden voyage. Ian emptied his glass in one, zipped up his flying jacket and put on his cap and goggles. He climbed aboard, pulled the canopy shut, strapped himself in and signalled to the pilot he was ready for take off. The tow plane revved its engines and set off down the runway at a steady pace. Behind it the glider skimmed along, barely touching the ground as if impatient to be set free. It took off as if it weighed no more than a butterfly.

At 3000 feet, he signalled to the pilot of the plane ahead he was about to release the tow rope and felt himself drift free. For a while he coasted around, seeking out the thermals that would take him higher. It was a perfect day for flying, good visibility and just the right weather conditions. He pressed first one rudder pedal then the other, astonished by the plane's responsiveness and agility. Whether he swerved, banked, put her into a steep climb or sudden drop she leapt to his command as if, defying gravity, she was attuned only to her natural element, the air. Never before had he experienced such a feeling of oneness with a plane. Like a living creature, he felt that if he handled her right there was nothing he could not ask of her as together they rode the sky.

'Dad, you're a genius,' he shouted to the empty air and for that moment forgave him everything.

He banked again but as he prepared to loop out on the last phase of a clover leaf, the plane caught a sudden downdraft and dived so hard the G-force took his breath away. Eventually he managed to arrest her fall and pull her back up but failed to reach more than 2500 feet, no matter how he tried. It wasn't the plane's fault. It was his for not handling her right. No doubt that would come in time. But the euphoria with which he'd started out was gone and the spell of unity broken. The awareness of his own clumsiness was proof, if that were needed, of the power of gravity. Its imperceptible threads, no matter how high he soared, held him earthbound like invisible steel hawsers. Only if he climbed high enough to reach a point of weightless balance between earth and air might it be possible to break earth's hold and at last sail free.

Face upturned towards the sky Dave watched his plane drift and swoop through the air, whilst the mechanic continued a running commentary on its performance. For once Dave was silenced. In his imagination he was up there with his son, putting his creation through its paces and marvelling at its grace. His son, of course, was too inexperienced to do it justice, though he would learn. He would pay for lessons and encourage him in every way he could. It would be no hardship. He couldn't think of a nicer way to spend a fine Sunday afternoon.

Ian made a somewhat jerky landing and brought the plane to a halt. His father, released from his temporary silence, met him with a barrage of questions which continued on the way home. Ian did his best to satisfy him, though the pressure in his head was mounting. As soon as they got home, he made an excuse and went to his room. He lay on his bed, staring at the ceiling and fighting to calm the chaos in his brain. He would have to find a way to stop his father from accompanying him every time he visited the airfield. Otherwise a wonderful gift would turn into a fetter, an albatross around his neck.

All week he thought about how to keep his father at home the following Sunday. But by Wednesday Dave was already planning the picnic they were to take with them and suggesting a course of more advanced flying lessons. Ian hadn't seen his father in such good spirits since he could remember. Any attempt to put him off would come as a bitter rejection and the last thing he wanted was to hurt him or seem ungrateful. On the other hand, he felt scarcely able to breathe and longed for the silence and emptiness of space.

By Saturday he still hadn't come up with a good enough excuse and reconciled himself to their going together to the airfield. He had, however, a plan for the following weeks. He would offer his services to his boss for stock taking or doing deliveries on a Sunday, in return for a day off during the week. Meanwhile he did his best to curb his resentment and concentrate his thoughts on the new glider. His father had taken to using the word 'we', as if they shared a joint existence like Siamese twins. In response Ian resorted to his childhood habit of conducting an imaginary game of catch, in which he ignored the ball his father repeatedly lobbed at him to show he wasn't playing.

At the airfield the mechanic spoke mostly to his father. Ian struggled to contain his rage and to stop himself from storming off. It was as much as he could do to force himself into the glider as they hovered over it, discussing its previous performance and his handling of it as if he wasn't actually present. Not until he had left the ground and looked down onto their ever-diminishing figures was he able to shed his anger like a snake soughing off an old skin.

It was a fine day with few clouds moving swiftly across the sky and so quiet he could hear the larks singing. He felt the glider eager to get free so he gave her her head. It was she who was in charge, he merely her custodian. He marvelled at her ability to nose her way by some unerring instinct into the thermals so that they rose higher and higher. Never had flight seemed so effortless. He lost all sense of time and gave himself up to the thrill of riding the air currents, as if the glider were made of nothing more solid than light. The world below was a mirage and the only reality this ethereal realm of space and sky.

The higher he rose the calmer he became and eventually a new thought occurred to him. Perhaps, after all, his father was not the weak tyrant he saw him as but a true visionary, who had envisaged the ultimate possibilities of flight. The more he considered it, the more that seemed the only convincing reason for his having built such a plane.

He recalled a story his father had read to him as a child. It was from a book of Nordic folk tales where the people believed the earth was enclosed by an invisible membrane like a giant caul. Each spring they sent up kites, which were really unmanned gliders, in an attempt to break through the membrane because after a hard winter it was at its weakest. The kites had sharp points on their tips so when they encountered it, they would make a small tear and those tears appeared as the brightest stars. Once, one of the kites broke right through the membrane and was never seen again. All that was left was the tail, which fell to earth. The kite belonged to the youngest boy in the village and was recognised by the eagle feathers and a piece of coloured leather the boy had attached to it. The story haunted him and he thought it might even be true that if you flew far enough, you could break through to some other dimension. Then there would be no limits to how far you could travel.

Dave and the mechanic waited for the glider's return. As darkness fell they continued to search the sky for signs of it. Hours had passed since it took off and they were starting to panic. They told themselves it was possible Ian had come down in a field somewhere and hadn't managed to get to a phone. But the terror Dave felt rose from his chest into his throat and threatened to choke him. The plane was too light and his son too inexperienced. He should never have let him take it up alone without an instructor. In his impatience to see what both of them were capable of, he'd pushed the boy too far before he was ready and now he was paying for it.

At seven thirty with the light gone, the mechanic announced he was going to scour the area in his van. He instructed Dave to man the phone in the office and alert everyone in the club phonebook to keep an eye out. Dave's mouth was dry and he whispered for help to the God he'd so long denied.

'Please, Lord! Take my life, if that is what you want. A life for a life, a fair exchange since it was my pride that brought this about. I was thinking more of my own prowess than of my son. I do not ask forgiveness!'

It was getting late but he did not put on the light. At last the phone rang. He snatched up the receiver. It was the mechanic.

*　*　*

'They'd found something, you see. Just beyond Collier's Wood near the quarry.'

The old man's voice quavered slightly as he told his tale for the umpteenth time.

'A plane wreck?' Francis prompted.

He shook his head.

'Just a cap and a pair of goggles. No glider and no body. They kept on looking but nothing more was ever found. They'd simply disappeared.'

He fixed Francis with his watery gaze.

'That young man was my son.'

Pig Woman

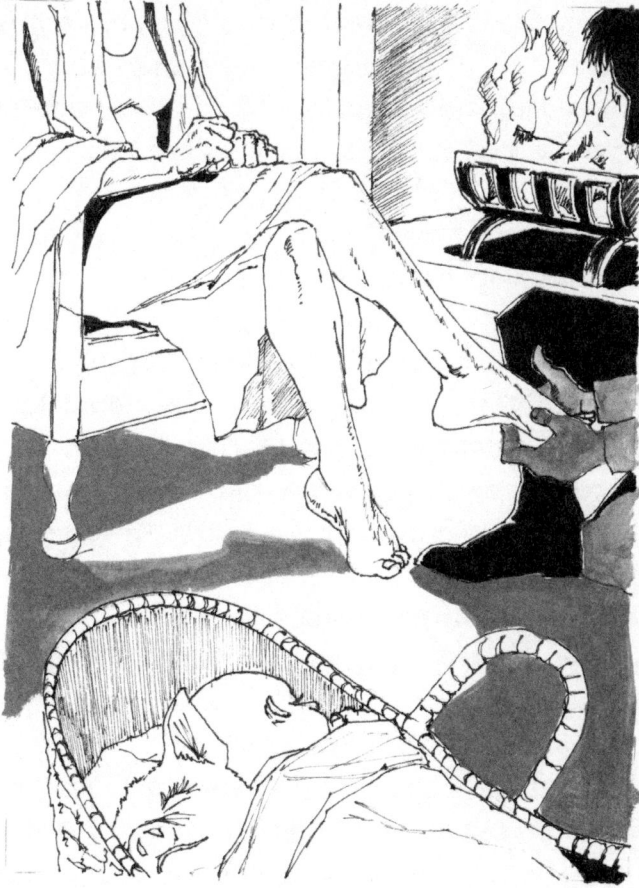

The young man picked up his pint and sandwich and sought refuge in the garden. After a warm summer, the grass there was worn bare by trampling feet and the tables littered with crisp packets and overflowing ashtrays. But at least he didn't have to listen to the crazy talk of that old man going on and on about time and the fourth dimension. He'd taken to spending his days in the pub to escape his own four walls, only to find himself victim of all those others with time on their hands and no one to talk to. It was like being stuck in a lift with a bunch of strangers, for whom the situation offers a longed-for opportunity of a captive audience.

The crisis in his own life had occurred when the legal case he and his team of social workers had been working on for two years collapsed. They had set out to expose a child pornography ring and had been working in close cooperation with the police. When a court hearing was finally called, the defence lawyers proved the police evidence insufficient for conviction and accused Social Services of conducting a witch hunt. The tabloid press, with their usual self-righteousness, launched a hate campaign against interfering and incompetent social workers, which put a stop to any thoughts of reopening the case.

The whole department was left demoralised. But for John it was worse, a personal failure, since he had under his care two children from one of the families known to be at the centre of the ring. Three generations of people whose natural feelings had dwindled to a single desire – a sadistic pleasure in exercising power over those weaker than themselves, including their own children. The worst thing was that he had as good as promised the children he would protect them. He knew this went beyond the bounds of professionalism but when he saw the hope that flickered in their small pinched faces he would have promised them anything.

Now through his own and his colleagues' failure, they were further than ever from deliverance and he had discovered that there was no point in trying to protect anyone from the trauma of abuse. All it took was a few fancy lawyers to overturn justice and twist the law in whatever way they chose.

The doctor said he was undergoing some sort of breakdown and prescribed tranquillisers. He was given leave of absence for six months and refused to take the tranquillisers. He needed to savour the full penance of his failure. The relationship with his girlfriend, already buckling under the strain, went into terminal collapse so he decided to use the period of solitary inactivity to see if he could turn himself into the painter he'd always hoped to become. That time was now over and he had reached the depressing conclusion that he lacked the focus and dedication necessary for a real artist. The world was overstocked with mediocre artists and he had no intention of adding to them. So when by the morning post he received the offer of a job in a city further north, he made up his mind to give it another shot. He still believed in social work as an honourable profession and it was high time he went back to earning a living.

He arrived in Nottingham and was greeted by his new boss, wearing a Hawaiian shirt under his suit jacket. The man's deliberately informal manner as he waved a letter of recommendation from his previous employment in front of John suggested his choice of dress was a gesture of defiance rather than a fashion statement. After the usual formalities, the boss explained that things were done a little differently up here and he should look upon the change as a chance to forget the past and start over. The first thing to realise was that a messiah complex was an occupational hazard of social work, especially amongst newer recruits. What was needed was the ability to compromise, to work for small adjustments and to keep in mind that useful psychotherapeutic term, 'good enough'.

His job initially was working with delinquent adolescents and he found it relatively easy to build up a good rapport with most of them. He'd been a tearaway himself and knew how it felt to be sixteen and a mixture of bored and terrified by your own imaginings. After a few weeks he was feeling more confident and even beginning to enjoy work again. Then on the retirement of one of his colleagues, he was assigned a case involving a child protection order. His first instinct was to refuse and he spent a sleepless night filled with bad dreams. In the morning, however, his confidence returned. It wasn't up to him to pick and choose his cases, and if he couldn't handle anything involving children he wasn't fit for the job.

The court had decreed the removal of an infant from its mother into the temporary, and possibly permanent, care of social services. Glancing over the thick file of notes he'd been handed, John saw she had already had a child taken from her four years previously and began to experience a familiar gnawing sensation in the pit of his stomach. He reminded himself that in this case no lawyers were involved and the court had already pronounced judgement, but the anxiety refused to let go.

He mentioned his new assignment to a couple of colleagues when they went to the pub for a beer and sandwich at lunchtime and one of them said with a smile, 'So they've given you the Pig Woman? Well, good luck, mate!'

The other grinned but neither of them would say what was funny. Eventually he gleaned from another member of the team, who'd been a friend of the man previously in charge of her case, that the woman was a notorious slag who lay down in a ditch with anyone drunk enough not to care. In an effort to help her, his colleague had tried to get her sterilised after the birth of her last child, obviously without success. When John asked if anyone else had actually seen her or been out to her place, he was told they had not. Rumour had it their colleague had developed rather a soft spot for her and that was one of the reasons for him quitting his job.

'She can't have been that ugly then,' John said.

His remark was received with general mirth and though he knew he was being teased for the rookie he was, it only added to his anxiety. A couple of days later he set out for the Burwell Hills, where the woman lived.

It was a cold day in late January, the very dead of winter. A low mist hung over the empty fields and by three o'clock as he was nearing his destination, what little light there had been was already fading. The heater in John's old Ford wasn't very effective and he could feel his toes growing numb in his too tight work lace-ups. He also suspected he'd lost his way.

Seeing a tractor crossing the field up ahead, he hailed the driver as it drew parallel and asked him for directions to the cottage. The farmer, whose countryman's face was even redder in the cold, told him to turn right at the end of the lane onto an unmade road then carry on for a couple of miles to the end. He asked John whether he was from the Council and when he admitted he was, the man declared it was about time something was done about that place. It was a scandal it should be let fall into such a state of disrepair. The woman had no right living there when bona fide farm workers were desperate for accommodation. John asked if he knew her but he shook his head. She didn't mix with locals, though he'd run into her a couple of times in the woods, scuffling around in the undergrowth looking for sticks or mushrooms. In her old coat and worn down boots, he'd taken her at first for an old sow. John asked how long she'd lived there and the man replied a good few years, ever since the estate was broken up and sold off. Her father had been gamekeeper, before the owner went away leaving his wife in charge. The place was now a ruin and the people who'd bought it were just waiting for it to fall down so they could build holiday homes.

The man would have gladly gone on talking all afternoon but John bid him a hasty goodbye and continued on his way. He turned off the road and drove slowly up the rutted track, taking care to avoid the deepest troughs where the mud had turned to ice. When he reached the end he saw a cottage standing alone in a patch of garden, surrounded by a stout picket fence. The place had settled into the land until it resembled some natural outcrop of rock. Part of the thatched roof had fallen in at one end and was covered by a sheet of corrugated iron. Except for a thin plume of smoke rising from the chimney, it might have been deserted.

As John got out of the car and opened the gate, a huge spotted sow emerged as if from nowhere and charged at him, stumbling in its haste and snorting with all the fury of a watchdog. Terrified, John stepped off the path and sank ankle-deep into the half-frozen mud. The front door opened and a harsh voice rapped out an order. The sow stopped in its tracks then turned towards the figure in the doorway. The woman, as she turned out to be, stepped forward and delivered a hefty slap on its mighty rump. The beast waddled off round the side of the house as John did his best to scrape the mud off his shoes on the edge of the path and to brush down his mackintosh. He heard a chuckle from the direction of the doorway, which increased his feeling of irritation. He was in no mood to be put off.

As he neared the house, he got a better look at the woman. She was bundled up in a man's waistcoat over a flannel shirt, thick wool skirt and on her feet a pair of men's boots with woollen socks turned down over the tops. A once fine paisley shawl was wrapped around her head and shoulders and almost masked her face, so that all John could see of it was one piercing black eye and a cheek like a withered apple. It was impossible to tell her age but one thing he was sure of, she was too old to be the mother of a young baby.

Daylight had by now almost disappeared and the only light from inside the cottage came from an oil lamp in the living room.

'I'd like to speak to Miriam Smith,' he said, holding out his identification.

The woman barely glanced at it.

'I believe she and her child are living here. I'd like to talk to her.'

'There's no child here,' the woman retorted.

Her voice was low but strong and there was nothing submissive about her.

'And the mother?' he persisted.

'There's no child and no mother.'

She went to shut the door in his face but he prevented her with his foot. Miriam Smith might have left as soon as she had received the court notice, but at least this woman probably knew something about her whereabouts.

'I'd like to come in and see for myself, if you don't mind.'

She hesitated for a moment then stood aside.

He entered and found himself in the living room. Apart from the single oil lamp, the fire gave off a flickering light. He tensed as he became aware of another presence moving stealthily along the wall behind him, then realised it was his own shadow. As his eyes got used to the gloaming, he took in a shabby but cosy room. There was an old armchair, with the stuffing hanging out, covered by a colourful handmade quilt, a table with two upright chairs and a rocking chair. A clothes rack was suspended from the ceiling and next to the fireplace was a stack of wood, with a bundle of half whittled sticks propped up next to it. An old dog lay asleep on the rag rug in front of the fire and on the far side was a basket, which at first he thought contained a couple of puppies under a blanket. But when he looked closer he saw that what was curled up there was not puppies but piglets. There was no sign of a baby.

He asked if he could take a look upstairs and she replied that she never used that floor, especially in winter, but he was welcome to do so if he wished. Upstairs consisted of a single room running the length and breadth of the cottage, a dormitory with inbuilt box beds where the farm labourers had once slept. At one end slivers of sky were visible through the rotted thatch and the place smelt of damp and must. He shivered at the clammy cold.

Re-entering the living room the heat and the sour smell of peat, mingled with the faint aroma of his own sweat, made him feel slightly sick. He undid his mac and asked the woman for a glass of water. As she went into the kitchen to fetch it, he cast around for any signs of a child. He could see no cot or toys and there were no baby clothes amongst the garments on the clothes rack. Either the office had got it wrong or, more likely, the woman had got wind of his visit and fled. He glanced through the half open door into the kitchen and caught sight of an ancient gas cooker and old-fashioned sandstone sink with brass taps, from one of which the woman was filling a glass with water. Hygiene, he suspected, was another reason this was no place fit for a child.

She returned and handed him the water, which he sipped taking care to let his lips touch the glass as little as possible. He opened his briefcase and fished out a copy of the court letter, explaining that it was an order to remove the child residing at this address into the temporary care of Social Services. The mother would have to attend a court hearing and, of course, would have the right to appeal. He handed the document to the woman but she made no move to take it, so he laid it down on the table.

'I already told you,' she said, 'there's no child here.'

'We have witnesses, who say that a woman and her baby have been living here. If you know where they are, you'd be well advised to tell me. For their sake.'

'If it's children you want,' the woman said curtly, 'try the big house on the main road. Calls itself a Children's Home. You'd make better use of your time inspecting that place.'

'It doesn't fall under my jurisdiction,' he replied, aware how pompous he sounded.

She gave a snort of contempt. He closed up his briefcase and gestured at the paper on the table.

'If she's your daughter or someone you know, better make sure she reads it. It'll be the police who call here next time.'

'If you want my daughter to read it, you'll have a long wait!'

He buttoned up his mac and made for the door.

'This place isn't fit for human habitation!' he said as a parting shot.

Outside, the cold had intensified and came as a shock after the oppressive warmth of the cottage. It was now dark. Clouds covered the stars and there was an eerie silence as before a storm. He shut the front door behind him, turned up his collar and fumbled in his pocket for his gloves. He raised his head as a faint cry came from the direction of the house. At first he put it down to the wind but he stood for a moment, listening. It came again and this time it was unmistakable - the cry of a baby. Instinct told him to ignore it, to get into his car and drive back to civilisation. But he knew that if there was a baby hidden in that cottage, it was his duty to find it. He turned back and rapped on the front door.

There was no answer so he hammered again. Still none. He put his shoulder against the door and it gave way without much difficulty. As he entered the living room he could hear the crying quite clearly. The old woman was standing by the fireplace, cradling in her arms one of the squealing piglets which was wearing what looked like a baby dress. He gazed in astonishment at its contorted pink face, toes crisped in rage and plump flailing arms as the realisation sank in that what the woman was holding was not a piglet but a human child.

'My God!' he exclaimed under his breath.

The woman wrapped the enraged baby in the blanket from the basket and sat down in the rocking chair. She turned her back to him, cradling the child in her lap. The crying ceased, broken only by faint sounds of animal-like contentment. John stared in disbelief at the woman's bent back. There could be no doubt about it. The child was feeding at her breast.

He reached for the water glass he'd left on the table and took a long swig, doing his best to shut his ears to the increasingly vigorous suckling. It made him nauseous just thinking about it. He did his best to concentrate on the crackling of the fire and the old dog groaning in its dream. It wasn't just the thought of the old woman's body, but worse still, a human child lying down with a pig. Any qualms he had had about taking it vanished at a stroke.

He sat down on an upright chair and tried to get a grip on himself. Seizing the child would not be easy. The woman was tall and, despite her age, he could see she was strong. She would prove more than a match for him if it came to defending her offspring. The best thing was to try to gain her confidence, then take her by surprise.

'How old is it?' he asked, as calmly as he could.

'She. She's five months.'

He still didn't believe she was the mother. Women, like cows, probably went on producing milk forever as long as they were suckled. He searched for some neutral topic of conversation and his gaze lighted on the bundle of whittled sticks next to the fireplace.

'Are you making something with those?'

She turned her head to follow his pointing finger and he caught sight of a cheek, flushed now like a withered apple.

'Brushes.'

'What sort of brushes?'

'Paint brushes, for artists. I make them with hazel or beech wood and hog hair. People come from all over the country.'

He noted the pride in her voice.

'So you're quite famous then!'

'It keeps me from the clutches of officials like you.'

Sensing the aggression in the air, the baby left off suckling and fussed with little snuffling cries. The woman lifted it to her shoulder and patted its back. A milky bubble ballooned from its pink mouth and it gave a satisfied burp. The woman bent her head and kissed its face then settled it back to its feeding.

John was starting to sweat.

'Take off your coat,' she said, as if sensing his discomfort though she had not looked at him. 'She'll be a while yet.'

Despite an instinctive reluctance, he took off his mac and laid it carefully over the back of his chair then undid the top button of his shirt and loosened his tie.

He was wearing his work suit but since he only had one, it had to do for summer and winter and wasn't very thick.

He glanced at the bundle of whittled sticks and memory flooded back: a white schoolroom with blue lino floor and pots of brightly coloured poster paints lined up in front of a blank sheet of paper. He was sitting cross-legged on the floor and as he picked up the brush to make the first stroke excitement overwhelmed him.

'I wanted to go to art college when I left school,' he heard himself say. 'But my parents felt university was a better preparation for a career.'

He regretted it at once. It sounded as if he had no mind of his own.

'You could paint, if that's what you want.'

'Being a Sunday painter never interested me.'

'If that's your excuse.'

He wanted to explain that he'd tried to be a proper artist, because dabbling in water colours on his day off was intolerable to him. All he had proved was that he lacked the necessary talent.

He glanced over to the window. It had started to snow and a flurry of white flakes struck the glass with a light thud. If he didn't leave soon, he wouldn't make it down that rutted track. The woman followed his gaze.

'Wait a while. It may stop.'

He heard the note of pleading in her voice and for the first time felt a twinge of compassion for what he was about to do. But it went as quickly as it had come.

'I'll make us a cup of tea while you finish feeding her,' he offered.

'Suit yourself.'

He got up and went into the kitchen. It was lit by a gas lamp attached to the wall and was cramped and untidy but not as dirty as he had feared. He found a chipped brown teapot and two pretty china cups without saucers and placed them on a tray with a picture of Harlech castle. He added a jug of milk covered with a piece of beaded muslin, and carried it into the living room.

'It's not wise taking a child out on a night like this,' the woman said, as he set down the cup on the floor beside her. 'Better wait till morning.'

'By morning, you'll be gone.'

He wasn't that naïve.

'Then stay here and make sure we aren't.'

'You know I can't do that.'

He gazed over at the window again.

'I'll give it a bit longer and see if the snow gives over.'

The heat in the room was becoming oppressive and he took off his jacket so that he was down to his shirt-sleeves, then sat down again and sipped his tea.

'It's just you and the child then?' he said conversationally.

'As you see.'

If she would be a bit more cooperative, they might work something out which would make the situation easier for both her and the child, he thought. The way she veiled herself in that old shawl wasn't helpful either, never looking him in the face, as if she was hiding something.

'Aren't you hot?' he said.

She gave a derisive laugh, as if she saw right through him.

'I'm just trying to be civil. Since we're stuck here for a while.'

An uneasy silence resumed, until suddenly she said,

'If you like, I'll tell you a story.'

'A story? What about?'

'You've heard of the Old Woman Who Lived in a Shoe?'

'Please! I'm not one of your infants.'

She shrugged.

'Very well. Go on, then.'

It would pass the time and might help to relax things.

'This cottage once belonged to the estate next door. There was a big house. A huge mock gothic monstrosity all fake turrets and gables. It burned down.'

She spoke with a light Derbyshire accent but her way of speaking was not that of a simple countrywoman. The more he knew of her, the more this woman confused him.

'The last owner, like the house, was full of pride and loved playing the big shot. He lived there with his wife, they had no children, and filled the place with old furniture and paintings of dead people he claimed to be related to.

'One day he disappeared and was never seen again. No one knew whether he'd been killed or done a bunk. There were rumours of gambling debts and shady deals. Whatever the truth of it, the money was gone. His wife lived on alone in the house without servants, who had left because there was nothing to pay them with. Except for what remained of the furniture and paintings, she was without a penny, so bit by bit she began selling them off too. Mostly she lived off the vegetables she grew and game bought cheap from a poacher. The local kids used to sneak in to play in her garden and she didn't shoo them away. Sometimes they helped her with her vegetable patch. Whatever friends she'd had deserted her when her husband left so she was no doubt glad of the company.

'Soon kids who'd run away from home, or had no homes to go to, got wind of the place and began staying over. There were plenty of bedrooms. The people in the village called her the Old Woman Who Lived in a Shoe after the nursery rhyme, though in actual fact she was not yet forty.

'At first the locals were quite sympathetic, seeing how her husband had run off like that. But soon they came to resent their kids spending so much time with her and complained about her influence over them. There were rumours of sex and drugs. Why else, they said, would kids be so attracted to the place?

'From being the Old Woman Who Lived in a Shoe, she turned into more of a Pied Piper, who they believed enticed their children with drugs instead of music.

Eventually one of the parents, a local magistrate, got a court order against her. But when the police arrived to search the place the kids escaped out of the windows and down the fire escape so the police found nothing, not even a syringe or the remains of a spliff. All the parents could do was threaten their brats with curfews and cutting off their pocket money - in a few cases boarding school.

'Some of the kids whose parents had called in the authorities told their social workers their main reason for going to the house was to seek refuge from parental neglect. One or two even mentioned abuse, and at this point enquiries ceased abruptly. People feared a witch hunt, with parents being subjected to hours of police grilling and no way to prove their innocence.'

The woman fell silent and turned her attention once more to the baby. It lay abandoned in a milky trance, its downy head flopped to one side, and seemed to be falling asleep.

'So what happened to her, this Pied Piper?' John asked.

'There was a fire. No one was seriously hurt but one night the place burned to the ground. The insurance company managed to avoid paying out on grounds of the premium being in arrears and the property not properly maintained. Apparently the wiring was old and had already been pronounced dangerous. She was convicted to two years suspended prison sentence for endangering the safety of minors in her care. No one ever saw her again.'

The story ended abruptly. John waited, but she said no more. He glanced at his watch. If he left right away, he might still get back to town and see the child settled in at the Children's Home before the main carers went off duty. But fear nagged at him. What if the car got stuck in a drift and he was forced to walk through the freezing dark with a tiny infant in his arms? What if he was responsible for it catching cold, or even dying? Outside, the snow was settling, covering the house in a protective blanket.

Inside the room, the child had fallen asleep. He got up.

'If she's finished feeding, we must go,' he said.

'Give me a moment,' the woman said, her voice suddenly soft. 'I'll wash her clothes and they'll be dry in no time in front of the fire. I can't send the little mite off with nothing.'

She stood up and for a second he caught a glimpse of the side of her face she'd kept hidden as she readjusted her scarf. He fancied it looked different, less lined, and it crossed his mind that she might be scarred from burns, perhaps in the fire she'd described, for he felt sure she had something to do with that house.

'Well?' she said.

'How can I trust you won't then make up some further excuse?'

'That's something you have to decide for yourself.'

'Forget it.'

He wasn't here to negotiate with her. He had a job to do and he meant to carry it out.

'Give me the child. We're leaving now.'

He got up and stretched out his arms so that she had to twist aside to keep the infant out of his reach. As she did so her unbuttoned shirt pulled apart, revealing a smooth breast with its dark, distended nipple. As John stared at it, an automatic stab of desire shot through him and he had to stop himself from stretching out his hand to touch the soft skin. He looked away quickly. How could he possibly want to touch this woman?

He remembered his mobile phone, pulled it out of his pocket and pressed the office emergency number. But the dial face on the phone remained blank and he realised there was no signal. In frustration, he flung the phone down onto the table. The old dog growled in alarm and the woman drew the baby to her.

He did his best to think calmly. Losing his temper was no good and only underlined the weakness of his position. He might as well face it, if he tried to take the baby out of here tonight there'd be a struggle, and even if he made it as far as the car, he'd probably end up in a snow drift. The only sensible option was to wait until morning. At least that way he could make sure they didn't run off.

The woman seemed to read his thoughts.

'You'll stay?'

'I don't have much option, do I?'

'Are you hungry?'

He realised he was starving. He hadn't eaten since breakfast.

She took down a clean blanket from the rack, wrapped the baby in it and carried it back to the basket by the fire. As she settled it down again, the piglet rolled over, stretching out its neat pink trotters with a sleepy grunt of pleasure. John swallowed down his protest. He wasn't here to offer advice on child care.

'It's not pigs as are filthy,' the woman said. 'It's human beings make them so.'

She went into the kitchen. He went on gazing at the two sleeping creatures lying side by side in the basket and his assumptions of normality slipped another notch. He had to admit there was a curious affinity between them, even the noises they made. The fire was making him sleepy and he wondered how was he going to get through this night.

The woman returned with a plate of stew and a jar of homebrew. She set a place at the table and invited him to sit down. It crossed his mind that she might have added some toxic mushrooms to the stew with the intent of poisoning him but he was too hungry to care. If she wanted to harm him there were plenty of ways to do so.

She went back to the kitchen and he ate ravenously as he listened to the sounds of water splashing in the sink. The food was good and in no time he had cleared his plate. The homebrew on the other hand tasted sour, though the after effect was warming and made him feel pleasantly tipsy. He poured himself a second glass from the jar and took it over to the armchair.

The woman re-entered, carrying a bundle of tiny wet garments which she hung out on the drying rack suspended from the ceiling. When she had finished, she sat down again in the rocking chair, pulled some sewing out of a cloth bag suspended from one of its arms and turned towards the lamp to thread her needle. Her wrinkled cheek seemed to belong to someone quite different from the owner of that smooth breast he'd glimpsed with its dark, distended nipple. He wondered if he'd imagined it and took another swig of homebrew.

'Why don't you go on with your story?'

'There's no more.'

'Shall I tell you what I think? I think maybe you were one of those children.'

She continued to sew in silence. Eventually she glanced up and he saw the look of critical appraisal in her dark gaze as if she were deciding whether or not he was a worthy listener.

'I was twelve when I went to live at the big house. My father looked after the horses on the estate but when they were sold with everything else, he fell into depression. Horses were his life, the only creatures he ever cared for. No doubt for that reason my mother had made off a few years earlier. I took to hanging round the kitchen, hoping for food, and noticing this, Madam, as everyone called her, took me in.

'There were about a dozen of us living there at the time, between the ages of three and twenty, boys and girls. I loved the place, its size and elegance, so unlike the cramped ugliness of our cottage. And, of course, I loved its freedom.

'Madam didn't exactly look after us or involve herself much in the everyday running of the household. She was like a queen bee presiding over her hive and we were left to fend for ourselves, with the help of a woman from the village and an old man once employed as gardener. The chores we shared between us. Even the smallest had to help out. But we could choose what we did, cook, clean or work in the garden. If you didn't work, you didn't eat. Persistent offenders were threatened with ejection, but the threat was rarely carried out and on the whole our little commune functioned well. Apart from our duties, we did pretty much what we liked.

'I, like most of the kids, admired and loved Madam from afar. None of us could understand how that husband of hers could go off and leave such a woman. Sometimes I imagined he hadn't left at all but she'd got rid of him and buried him somewhere in the woods. Poverty, I considered, would be a small price for her freedom.

'Occasionally, either as a reward or just because she felt like it, she gave us presents. For my thirteenth birthday she gave me a beautiful pair of red shoes. I remember putting them on and coming down the grand staircase in a trance of happiness. Held in a spotlight of sunshine from the domed window above, I felt like a princess. I saw nothing but my red shoes as they descended, step by step.'

She paused for a moment and her hands fell idle in her lap. Then she picked up her sewing and resumed her story.

'Every hive, as you know, has its drones as well as its workers. Not all the workers were female and not all the drones male, though most were – lustful young men keen to flex their muscles and impose their will and do the minimum when it came to sharing out the chores. They hid their desire for the forbidden queen for fear of expulsion and turned instead to lesser females. At thirteen I was beginning to attract their attention. I made myself as invisible as I could and did my best to avoid being alone. But that day of my birthday, as I descended the stairs in my red shoes in the shaft of bright sunlight, I forgot all danger and displayed myself in all my young glory.

'One of the drones had seen me and was waiting at the foot of the stairs. I felt his hands on my shoulders and his strong breath on my cheek. As I raised my head, I saw the wolf's gleam in his eyes and tried to pull away. But his grip tightened and he dug his fingers painfully into my collar bones. I lowered my eyes from his gaze, hardly daring to breathe. Then I heard footsteps, Madam's high heels clicking smartly across the tiled floor of the hall. 'I've seen you,' he hissed in my ear before sliding away into the shadows, and I knew my fate was sealed.

'I hid my new shoes and later that day when I was working in the herb garden, my favourite refuge, Madam came to me. She was wearing a light summer frock, long out of fashion, but still she looked as elegant and sophisticated as someone at a garden party. It was one of those lovely evenings when, after a dull day, the clouds clear and for a brief hour the sun breaks through before setting. My heart was full of love at the sight of her. She said she hoped I was enjoying my birthday and that Gussy had baked me a cake, which would be presented after supper. She must have sensed my fear because she began talking about being thirteen and the troubles as well as joys it brought and which I must prepare myself for. She dug in the small handbag she always carried with her and produced a pearl handled pocket knife, which she pressed into my hand. I said she'd already given me a birthday present but she shook her head. This was something special, she said, from her to me. 'If someone intends to harm you and won't heed you, you must protect yourself in whatever way you can.' And with that she walked away.

'I felt a thrill of danger. Things were worse than I had feared if Madam couldn't protect me, as her gift made clear. I knew how weak and vulnerable I was.

'Lately I'd graduated to a room of my own. But that night I left my bed and went to sleep with two of the younger ones. By day I worked in the garden, under the eyes of the old gardener, and the rest of the time kept myself out of sight as much as possible and did my best to stay alert for my predator.

'One hot afternoon during the heat wave of a late Indian summer, I'd had enough of working outside and came in to change out of my jeans and sweaty work shirt. As I turned the corner on the landing, I sensed his presence. Uncertain whether to make a run for it or seek the safety of my room, and too frightened to think clearly, I decided for my room. The door was open and by then it was too late to turn back.

'He slipped in after me and set his back against the door. My hand closed on the knife in my pocket as he came for me and shoved me onto the bed. He held me down, ripping my clothes in his haste. I wriggled one arm free, flicked open my knife single-handed in the way I'd practised and plunged it between his ribs. He gave a groan of surprise and pain as he collapsed on top of me. I couldn't move, expecting at any moment to be knocked out or strangled. But in a few moments I felt his body go limp. His head fell forward onto the pillow next to mine and his breathing grew hoarse and laboured. I could hardly breathe with the weight of him. My fingers felt a stickiness where I'd stuck the knife in and I knew it must be blood.'

She stopped speaking. John's body was inert but his mind was attentive. In the quietness of the room, he could hear the rhythm of his breathing.

'How did you explain the body?' he asked.

'Madam told the police there'd been a fight with intruders and the boy had been stabbed. Kids from the neighbouring villages often turned up looking for trouble. I'd hidden the pearl handled knife so, though they searched the place, the police would never find it. They questioned us, together with some of the village youths, but to no avail. No parents came forward to claim their son and the case was getting nowhere. But the reputation of the house as a source of trouble was growing.

'It was October and the days were getting cold. One night the children were in bed and asleep but as usual I lay awake in the dark. I got up to open the window for a breath of night air and saw pin-points of light moving through the bushes on the far side of the lawn. As I watched, about half a dozen figures emerged from the trees and ran across the grass to the house. I dashed to the main staircase in time to hear the first crash of glass and saw through the open door the flash of petrol igniting. A missile landed in the room, followed by another then another. The brocade curtains caught light and soon flames were biting into the waxed floorboards. Pockets of fire scampered along the rugs, licking at the legs of chairs and tables. It was a windy night and soon the air was filled with fragments of burning debris. A scrap of brocade touched my cheek and settled into the collar of my nightdress, sending it up in a torch of flame. I tore it off and ran naked to the place where the hand bell, which summoned us at meal times, was kept and rang it for all I was worth.'

'You were hurt?'

She ignored him and continued her tale.

'Madam and old Tom, the gardener, were running through the house into every room, waking the children and carrying out those too sleepy to flee themselves. The older ones tried to help but were too stunned or frightened to be much use. Madam was tireless. If it hadn't been for her, things would have turned out very different.'

'No one was lost?'

She paused then said softly.

'One. A baby. She'd turned up on our doorstep a few days earlier, wrapped in a handmade blanket but with no note or anything to identify her. Grace, the woman who came to help out, had just fed her and put her to sleep in her basket next to the stove in the kitchen since it was a chilly night. It wasn't until everyone else had been accounted for that Madam suddenly realised she was missing. By then it was too late. The whole place was in flames. She tried again and again to get back into the house. In the end she had to be dragged away for her own safety. That was the last time I saw her.'

She stopped speaking and the only sound was the repetitive ticking of the clock. It was the dead of night. A log slipped in the fire, making a soft explosion and sending up a shower of sparks. Startled, the old dog raised his head, then settled back to sleep. From the basket on the other side of the fireplace came the softest whisper, the sweet breath of sleeping infants, light as a leaf. John leaned his head back against his chair and stretched out his legs. His limbs felt heavy and his eyes prickled with exhaustion. He longed to sleep but his mind would not be stilled. Fearful shadows from his own childhood stirred like sleepwalkers beneath the surface of his mind.

He must have fallen asleep because when he came to, he was shivering and a blanket had been placed over him. The woman was standing by the fire, pouring water from the big kettle into a glass already half full of some concoction. She handed it to him, telling him to drink it down. It would make him feel better. He held the glass between his hands, relishing its heat, and looked over at her. She was bending down to unlace her boots and easing them off her feet. Her shawl had slipped down to her shoulders and some strands of hair fallen forward, partly obscuring her face. She had removed her woollen skirt and baggy waistcoat in favour of a faded print dress.

He watched transfixed as, having removed her boot, she spread her toes like a cat that gets ready to clean between them. Her feet were dainty with high arches, unblemished by corn or bunion. They reminded John of his own when he was a child and went barefoot. That was before he took to wearing his cowboy boots day in, day out until they fell apart. He leaned forward and taking a foot in each hand, cupped them between his fingers like two delicate birds. The soles felt slightly rough but the cool blobs of the toes made him think of blackberries. Self-conscious, he released them again and sat back in his chair.

She was looking into the fire, half turned from him. The hair that was loosely gathered into the nape of her neck was a rich chestnut brown. He felt the ground slipping away. Nothing was as it seemed and he was all at sea. He gazed at her profile and saw the disfigurement that ran down her left cheek and disappeared into the neckline of her dress, the result no doubt of the burns she'd received that night when her nightdress caught fire. Terrible for a child of thirteen to carry such a stigma, her beauty destroyed before it had time to blossom!

'What's your name?' he asked softly.

She lifted her head and he caught his breath in wonder. The face she turned to him passed from blemish to beauty, features of such delicate proportion and skin smooth and unscarred. Her bright gaze reached into his very core, making his heart beat faster. It was as if she had transformed herself from an ugly larva into an exquisite butterfly, for him.

'Miriam,' she replied. 'What do you see?'

'The most beautiful woman in the world!'

She smiled and he wanted to weep at her loveliness.

'Will you leave me my daughter, John?'

Hearing his name on her lips gave him a stab of delight, though he didn't remember mentioning it. What did it matter if in the eyes of the authorities this woman was an unfit mother? She refused to be judged.

He got up and kneeling beside her, took her hands in his.

'You know others will come in my place. The only way to fight this is to challenge it in court. I haven't much money but I'll give you what I can, help you to prepare your case. There's no other way.'

The look in her eyes silenced him. Argument was useless. He reached out his arms and drew her close.

They kissed and, for the first time in a very long while, he felt whole. She stretched out along the hearthrug and pulled him to her. The beauty of her body as she removed her clothes astonished him and he entered her like a parched man slaking his thirst, knowing that he had come home.

The grey dawn reflected off the fallen snow and lit up the room with a deathly half-light. It was the biting cold that woke him as he lay on the hearthrug, naked except for a thin blanket. The fire had gone to ash and he knew at once, even before he opened his eyes, that he was alone. He sat up and looked about him. The basket was empty, the old dog no longer lay beside the fire and the woman and child were gone. He raised his head in silent agony. Like some wounded minotaur, he felt only rage at the unimaginable pain that consumed him. The heart had been torn from his chest and it was his own fault. She had offered him trust and he had talked of money and courts. He had left her no choice but to flee.

He flung off the blanket and ran out into the snow, floundering around like some mad creature until at length the frenzy passed and, bruised and frozen, he returned to the house. All day he sat in the rocking chair, wrapped in the quilt, waiting, though he knew she would not return. At last, when darkness fell, he got up and left the house. He had eaten and drunk nothing but he didn't think of that or anything else as he drove back to town through the melting snow.

For a week he was off sick and lay in his room with the curtains shut, oblivious to night or day, swallowing anything that promised oblivion. When eventually he got up and returned to work, people were shocked by his altered appearance. In the past he'd enjoyed a night out with the boys but wasn't considered a drinker. Now he drank after work with the aim of getting drunk. Sometimes it ended up in a fight so that colleagues began crying off or changing their meeting places to exclude him. He didn't care. He didn't care about anything.

Eventually, his line manager called him into his office and told him he'd better see a doctor and get sick leave since he was obviously unfit for work. John asked what would happen to his cases in his absence but his boss refused to discuss them. His priority, he said, was to get himself sorted out because with his previous reputation for collapsing under pressure, this was his last chance.

That lunchtime a couple of workmates accompanied him to the pub for a farewell drink. As they sat over their pints and sandwiches, he asked if either of them had heard anything about the 'Pig Woman' case or knew if it had been reassigned.

'I reckon they've given up on that one,' one of them replied.

'A mate of mine, who lives in a village up Burwell way, told a story,' the other said.

'Oh?'

He was all ears.

'He's just moved into a flat over a greengrocer's on the High Street,' the man went on. 'A couple of nights ago him and his missus are tucked up in bed, when they're woken by this God-awful racket. A car exhaust goes off right under the window like a firecracker and there's a mad shrieking from some crazy banshee. He gets up, goes to the window and what d'you think he sees?'

John shook his head impatiently.

'A beat-up old pickup is farting its way down the High Street and in the back is this massive old sow. Trotters up on the side and snout in the air, it's squealing fit to wake the dead and all ready to jump out. And this woman is leaning out the driver's window, cursing at it like a navvy. It was like something out of a Laurel and Hardy film, he said.'

'Which way were they headed?'

'I wouldn't worry. Whichever it was, she's someone else's headache now.'

The snow was almost gone and John set off for the Burwell Hills. It was colder away from the city and a few white traces still clung to the hedgerows and the hollows of fields, where the winter sun never reached. The going was hard along the frozen cart track and he had to take it slowly. When he pulled up outside the cottage, it looked more forlorn than ever. There was no smoke from the chimney and the only signs of life were a few frost bitten cabbages in the garden. He tried the front door but it was locked so he went round to the back and after a couple of shoves, the door gave way.

Inside it felt even colder, desolate in its neatness. There was no fire in the grate or colourful rugs in the lifeless sitting room. The place felt as abandoned as last year's nest when the birds have flown. He'd known in his heart that coming back was pointless. She wasn't the sort of person to leave a note or an address and probably didn't know where she was going.

He closed his eyes and tried to recall the room as it had been that night and the shock of her beauty, so flawed and so desirable. He tried to picture her body as they made love, but already reality was transforming itself into some imagined ideal. It seemed impossible to hang on to the flesh and blood of her, even as memory.

He wandered over to the empty basket where the child and the piglet had lain together and stared into it unseeingly. Through the fog of his gaze, he began to focus on something hidden in its recesses. He bent down and picked up a slim parcel wrapped in newspaper. He turned it over several times in his hands, before he could bring himself to unwrap it.

Inside were two paintbrushes, skilfully crafted out of beech wood. One was made of hog's hair, the other of something finer. He caught for a moment the sound of her voice, as she impatiently dismissed his excuse for giving up on his art because he refused to be merely a Sunday painter. He understood that her gift was a message, a gesture of faith and a command to action. It said that whatever label he chose to go by was of no importance, that it was time to stop prevaricating and get to work.

Yes, he would answer her challenge with all the skill and force of imagination of which he was capable. He would not fail her.

Grimalkin

S imon leaned forward and, with exaggerated care, set down his glass on the beer-stained table in front of him. He and Andy had been walking on the moors for several hours.

They had eaten nothing since breakfast and the drink had gone to his head. It was supposed to be a walkers' pub but you were requested to leave your muddy boots in the porch and the snug bar had been fitted with a sofa and some scuffed leather armchairs to resemble somebody's living room. Bookshelves lined the wall at either side of an inglenook fireplace, dead now because of the warm weather, and there were pictures for sale by local artists.

Andy returned with two more pints and a couple of bags of crisps and set them down in front of him.

'Christ! Give me a dart board and formica tables every time!'

He followed Simon's gaze to one of the pictures. It showed a woman, standing in a doorway. One hand shaded her eyes and she gazed along the empty road as if waiting for someone.

'You like that kitsch?'

'It's got something.'

'It's schmultz!'

'Like most songs. It doesn't necessarily mean they're bad.'

Andy sighed.

'It's fake, like the décor. But you never had any taste... Are we going to eat here or find somewhere else?'

Simon pointed to the wall above the bar.

'There's a menu on the board over there.'

The walk had worked up an appetite and after they'd eaten and Andy had fallen asleep, Simon's gaze returned to the picture. It unsettled him, like a half-forgotten memory. Then it came to him. The summer before last he'd been made redundant and was feeling useless and depressed. Someone suggested that rather than moping around the flat, he should try a change of scene and he'd decided to use up the last of his savings and take a train to Scotland to go walking.

He loved the Highlands. During his childhood, his family went every year to visit his mother's sister near Inverness, from where he'd set out to explore the countryside, first with his father and later on his own. The sense of freedom provided him with a longed-for feeling of liberation and the beauty of the landscape had etched itself into his consciousness. Even after his aunt died, he kept up regular visits. There was always a house or a B & B where he could spend the night.

On the third evening of this particular visit, it was getting late and there wasn't a dwelling or even a light as far as the eye could see. He was tired and hungry and began to fancy he'd be sleeping under a hedge, which without tent or sleeping bag wasn't a pleasant prospect. Then, as he rounded the brow of a hill, he saw below him a house. It was a solid, two-storey affair attached to a barn with a walled garden, a walnut tree and a row of pleached pears. It looked like a green oasis in an otherwise colourless landscape.

He walked up the path and knocked on the front door. It was opened by an old woman, so small and brown she reminded him of an oversized mouse. She was dressed very properly in a tweed skirt, Fair Isle pullover and well-polished brogue shoes, and wore her hair in a tight plait wound into a knot at the nape of her neck. Simon asked if she had a room he could rent for the night. She studied him for a moment then invited him in.

She showed him into a living room, filled with handsome furniture and three long windows looking out onto an abundant garden.

'We've had our tea but there's bread and goat's cheese and the first of our apples,' she said.

It sounded like a feast, so he thanked her and she told him to wait and she'd bring him a tray. When she had gone he wondered idly who 'we' might be, since there was no sign of anyone else in the house.

She sat with him as he ate but he was too hungry to be self-conscious. She asked what he was doing in that part of the world and he told her he enjoyed walking and had spent several holidays along this coast as a child. When he had finished eating she took the tray and announced she was off to her bed, since it was her habit to retire with the light and rise with it in the morning. If he was ready, she would show him to his room.

He had the impression that his bedroom had belonged to a child. Though there were no toys, the bed was narrow, the furniture under-sized and the curtains adorned with ribbons. The sheets smelt of camphor and were slightly damp but he fell asleep at once and remembered nothing further till he woke with the sun on his face, having forgotten to close the curtains. For a while he lay there, listening to the lazy clucking of a hen and the squeak of a door hinge as it swung back and forth in the yard below. From inside the room he could hear the slow creaking of a beam and a rustling curtain in the morning breeze. He felt relaxed, despite the bed being too short and his feet hanging over the edge. He had no idea of the time and might have lain there all morning but for the need to pee that forced him up.

He threw on his jeans and padded barefoot along the corridor. After a couple of closed doors, he found the third ajar and glanced inside. The room was large with a tall, leaded window. Someone, whom he took at first for a dwarf, was in the act of throwing back the heavy curtains to let in the morning light. It fell across the bed where a girl was sprawled, half covered by a rumpled sheet. She lay in a state of trance-like abandonment, one leg crooked, the sheet half fallen to the ground to reveal a small round breast with its rosebud nipple. Her hair, which was an astonishing shade of red, tumbled over the pillow.

She raised an arm to cover her eyes against the light and, as he shifted his gaze, he became aware of a third presence in the room. A huge, ferocious-looking black cat was squatting on the tallboy beside the window. Its malign yellow gaze appeared to be directed straight at him.

Ten minutes later, as he descended the stairs to the hall, the old woman called him into the kitchen. There was porridge and tea and she invited him to help himself then disappeared into the yard. He ate slowly, hoping the girl might appear to share his breakfast. The image of her sprawled there, languid and half-naked, aroused him and he tried to think up reasons for staying on. Eventually, as if in answer to his thoughts, the old woman returned and told him a tree had come down in the night. She had a chain saw and asked if he would cut it up in lieu of payment. He agreed.

He had never used a chain saw before and it gave him a satisfying sense of power, like a true man of the woods. At midday the old woman called him into the house, where she had laid out soup with hunks of homemade bread. But there was still no sign of the girl. She told him she had to drive to the village to deliver her eggs and if he finished the tree, there were some slates that needed replacing on the barn and a ladder beside it. It seemed to be accepted that he would stay another night.

He cut up the last of the tree and went indoors to get a drink. A female voice called out to him and he knew at once it was the girl. He followed the sound to the living room. She was seated on the sofa, legs drawn up primly beneath her and the cat on her lap, purring loudly. She looked up at him with a gaze that was strangely unfocussed so that he wondered for a moment if there was something wrong with her vision. Her eyes, in the pale oval of her face with its aureole of wild red hair, were of so vivid a blue they held him captive in their depths.

'Sit down,' she ordered.

'I didn't mean to disturb you. I came in for a drink.'

'In this place any disturbance is welcome.'

'You're bored?'

'Wildly and incandescently!'

He laughed.

'Do you live here all the year round?'

'No, thank God. I'm recuperating. Martha is looking after me. She used to be my nanny. This, by the way, is Grimalkin. The witch's cat.'

She scratched the cat under the chin and it closed its eyes in bliss.

'It was a bit of luck coming across this place last night. Otherwise it'd have been me and the stars,' he remarked in an attempt to match her extravagant tone.

'There used to be a village here once but there was a fire or plague or something and the people died or left. My father bought it as a holiday house. The local river has good fishing.'

'Where do you live normally?'

'You ask a lot of questions. Tell me something about yourself.'

He gave her a quick rundown of his life so far, aware he was making it sound far more interesting than it actually was. As he spoke she leaned forward and sniffed the air, like a blind man trying to catch his scent. There was something disturbingly feral about the gesture and to avoid her gaze he reached down to stroke the cat on her lap. She stretched out her fingers and ran the tips gently across his face. They felt cool and light as feathers and her nails scraped faintly against his skin, sending out tiny shocks like sparks. He closed his eyes and suddenly felt something rip across his cheek. When he put his hand to his face, he could feel blood.

'Vile creature!.. I'm so sorry. You'd better go and bathe your face. There's antiseptic in the bathroom cabinet.'

He went upstairs, unsure whether her casual manner or the savagery of her beastly cat enraged him more. Why hadn't she warned him it was vicious? He rinsed his cheek under the cold tap and when it had stopped bleeding descended the stairs and went out into the yard, fearing that if he saw the wretched creature again he'd be tempted to wring its neck. The incident had brought him to his senses. It was too late to leave that evening but first thing in the morning he'd be on his way.

When the old woman returned she laid out supper in the kitchen, but the girl did not appear and Simon was relieved. Martha became quite talkative. She told him she'd first come to work for the family when the father of her young charge, Isobel, was a boy, and described the holidays they'd spent together at the house. The doctor had ordered the girl several months of complete rest so they were due to remain here until Christmas. When Simon asked what was wrong with Isobel, she replied, 'Nothing, except she is too fine for this world.'

Her answer seemed irritatingly pretentious and destroyed at a stroke whatever sympathy he might be feeling for the girl.

That night he was woken from a sleep full of dreams by the sound of sobbing. His window was open and it seemed to be coming from somewhere in the garden. He pulled the blankets over his head and did his best to go back to sleep. Eventually, when it did not cease, he got up and went to the window. The garden was bright with moonlight but he could see no one out there. He pulled on his jeans and went into the corridor.

Uncertain where the old woman slept, or if the weeping might be coming from her, he tiptoed along the corridor making as little noise as possible. At the end he came to a flight of stairs and at the top there was a door, fastened by a latch. A pale light glowed from under it. He lifted the latch, opened it a crack, and looked in.

The room gave the impression of a kind of Aladdin's cave. It had a pitched roof and three mansard windows, through which the moon shone almost bright as day. A piece of cloth, woven with gold, red and silver threads depicting exotic birds and animals, had been thrown over a tailor's dummy and gleamed in the pallid light. Puppets, elaborately dressed and disturbingly lifelike, hung from the beams, and at the far end a stage had been erected, adorned with paper lanterns in which candles flickered in the light breeze. In the centre stood a loom, with a half-finished strip of the same exotic cloth that was draped across the dummy. Some of the threads had been violently wrenched out and the girl was leaning over it, slashing at the fabric with a pair of giant scissors.

Afraid she might turn her weapon on herself, Simon ran to her and grabbed her by the arm. She wrenched it free and with great, sobbing gasps, raised a clenched fist in which she gripped the scissors. The blank terror of her gaze made him think she didn't recognise him. He managed to twist aside at the last second as she lunged at him, almost stabbing him to the heart. Instead she ripped his teeshirt and slightly grazed his arm.

He seized her roughly and thrust her back against the frame of the loom, twisting her arm so that she dropped the scissors, which he kicked into a corner. He acted with such swift defensiveness that he might have done her real harm, if she hadn't gone suddenly limp in his arms and slumped to the floor. He crouched down beside her, afraid he'd hurt her. He could feel the beating of her heart within the narrow cage of her ribs, like a captured bird. His teeshirt was wet with a mixture of sweat and her tears but the fight had gone out of her.

He wiped the damp hair from her face, as the aftershocks of weeping shuddered through her. She was calmer now and her eyelids flickered closed but her arms gripped him tight. He stroked her back with his free hand. His supporting arm was getting pins and needles so he lifted her up and carried her over to the divan on the far side of the room. He was shocked by how light she was, despite her strength. He laid her down but she refused to let go of him, muttering repeated apologies. She hadn't realised it was him. She had confused him with someone else. He must tell her he forgave her violent attack. He reassured her as best he could that he wasn't hurt. She entwined her legs with his and bit by bit, as they lay there on the divan, reassurance turned into caresses that grew increasingly urgent.

He waited until he knew she was sleeping peacefully before extricating himself from her embrace. The moon had disappeared and it was now quite dark. As he pulled the quilt up over her, his hand encountered the curled form of Grimalkin lying in the crook of her knees. It must have sneaked in unnoticed. He quickly withdrew his hand, but the cat merely purred and he groped his way out of the room.

The next morning he awoke with a start as his bedclothes were flung aside and his clothes landed on top of him. He opened his eyes to see the old woman standing over him, her face contorted with fury.

'Evil snake! Here am I, building up her trust and you undo it all in a single night!'

He protested his innocence, insisting he'd done Isobel no harm. But she refused to listen.

'At fifteen that girl's seen more horrors than most of us in a lifetime! She doesn't need you.'

Rage gave the diminutive creature a kind of majesty.

'Fifteen?.. I thought she was … nineteen or twenty.'

'You thought!'

She spat in disgust.

Unwilling to encounter the old woman again and without waiting for breakfast, he packed his bag and wrote a note to Isobel, telling her he would write as soon as he got back to London. It was hard to believe that with all her sophistication, she was so young. If he'd known, he never would have let things come to such a pass. He left the note on the kitchen table, though he was pretty sure the old woman would destroy it before Isobel could read it. There was nothing else to be done since she certainly wouldn't let him near her.

As he reached the brow of the hill, he turned to look back down the road. The girl was standing beside a door in the garden wall, shading her eyes with one hand. Even from this distance he could feel the intensity of her gaze, like the beam of a laser. He waved but she didn't wave back. He doubted whether she could see much from so far away with her peculiar eyesight. For a moment he was unsure whether to go on or turn back, but at length he carried on over the brow of the hill until, when he looked back, the house was lost to view.

As Simon gazed at the painting on the wall of the snug bar, he realised that until that moment he'd scarcely thought of Isobel for over a year. When he'd first returned from Scotland, he'd thought of her often and wanted to send her a letter. But pursuing a relationship with a fifteen year old would only make trouble for both of them and he'd done his best to put her from his mind. Eventually the demands of his life and a new job had done the trick and she returned to him only in dreams, bending over him so that her long red hair brushed his face and he gazed up into that blue gaze that saw everything and nothing. Once, in a dream she'd handed him a suit of clothes and as he put them on, they'd stuck to him like a second skin. He'd become frantic in the effort to pull them off until with relief he woke up. But after a while even the dreams stopped.

Returning to London after the holiday with Andy, he resumed his life. But the rekindled memory of Isobel would not let him go. In September he had some holiday due and decided to revisit Scotland. The weather in August had been rotten but now the country was basking in an Indian summer and London was stifling. In the Highlands the hills would be purple with heather and the air full of lark song and the smell of the sea.

He took a train to Glasgow and then a bus, which brought him within a mile or so of the house. He walked the last of the distance and as he crested the hill it appeared below him in its green oasis. But as he drew nearer, he realised something was different. There were no lights on, though it was nearing dusk, and the garden looked overgrown and neglected. He mounted the steps, rang the bell and waited. He pressed it again several times then walked around the house. The living room windows were shuttered, with leaves piled up against them as though they hadn't been opened for months.

He heard a rustling sound in the bushes and a piteous meowing. Grimalkin emerged from the undergrowth and began rubbing himself delightedly against his ankles. When he bent down to stroke him, he could feel the bones beneath his previously sleek fur, rough now and matted with burrs. He wondered what could have made Isobel abandon a creature she'd once so cosseted. He searched inside his rucksack for some food and came up with a half eaten sandwich and an apple. He fished the tuna out of the sandwich and gave it to the cat, which seized it from his outstretched fingers then sat washing its face as if it had just enjoyed a royal banquet. It was then Simon noticed the collar, nestling against the scraggy fur of its neck. He bent down and, still wary despite the animal's apparent docility, carefully undid the buckle. Attached to the collar was a disc with the owner's name, an address in London and a phone number. He slipped it into his rucksack, gave the cat a final stroke and turned back the way he had come.

It wasn't until after Christmas, when he was clearing out his rucksack, that he came across the cat's collar. By now more than two years had elapsed since he'd first seen Isobel and his memory of her had grown vague. He reckoned she'd be seventeen or eighteen by now and wondered if she'd even remember him. What they'd had was no more than a one night stand but something about her continued to haunt him. So one crisp Sunday morning in February, he copied down the address on the cat's collar and cycled across town to the district where he presumed she lived.

The house was Edwardian and semi-detached, situated in a leafy street in a pleasant neighbourhood. He rode slowly past, took a turn around the block and pulled up on the far side of the street. He gazed across at the windows, hoping for a sight of Isobel but there was no sign of anyone. Eventually he leaned his bike against the hedge, climbed the steps and rang the bell. If someone answered, he'd claim to be a friend of hers from Scotland.

A tall man with grey hair, dark suit and an unwelcoming manner opened the door.

'Is Isobel in?'

The man blinked as if to clear the intruder from his sight.

'And who are you?'

His speech was strangely accented and deliberate in a way that might have been the result of a stroke.

'A friend from Scotland. I said I'd look her up when I was next in London.'

There was a pause then the man said,

'Sorry. She's not here,' and shut the door.

The fact that he hadn't actually denied Isobel lived there convinced Simon it was the right address. Perhaps she'd got a job, though that was hard to imagine, or carried out her ambition to go to art school. All he wanted, he told himself, was to apologise for abandoning her in such a cavalier fashion and to know she was all right.

During the following weeks, he cycled over several times in the evenings after work to keep watch on the house. He didn't phone, fearing to arouse the suspicions of the reptilian man and whoever else lived there. Once or twice he saw the man arrive home in his Mercedes, park and let himself into the house. Once a woman opened the door to him, but it wasn't Isobel.

He'd almost given up when one Sunday afternoon, as he turned into the street, he noticed a small brown figure emerge from the basement area of the house and scuttle off down the road. He recognised her at once and followed her on his bike. He slewed to a halt in front of her, blocking her path.

'Martha? It's Simon. Remember? You gave me a room a couple of summers back. In Scotland.'

She looked him up and down, startled and unsmiling.

'There's nothing wrong with my memory!'

'How's Isobel?'

'What's it to you? Go away!'

She turned and resumed her brisk walk. He pushed his bike alongside her, keeping pace.

'I don't mean any harm. I just want to know how she is.'

'Was it you who called at the house?'

'Her father told you? I assume that's who he is.'

'He said some undesirable was hanging about and warned us

not to speak to you.'

'Not a very friendly guy.'

'How did you know where we lived?'

'The cat you left behind in Scotland had a disc on its collar with the address.'

'Grimalkin?'

He nodded.

'I wonder you could just abandon the poor thing.'

'He hates London. He didn't want to be found'

'Isobel must have been upset.'

'She forgets quickly.'

Despite her prickliness, he could feel her softening.

'Tell me. Where is she?'

She turned to him and her wrinkled brown face crumpled into a hundred tiny folds.

'You really care about her?'

'I haven't been able to get her out of my mind.'

It was an exaggeration but it did the trick. She hesitated for a moment longer, then said, 'I'm on my way to see her now. You can come with me, if you like.'

The building they arrived at was a grim Victorian pile, one of the few asylums that hadn't yet been shut down.

Simon recognised it with a shock that for a moment almost paralysed him. He'd visited his mother there, or in some more or less identical place, during the last year of her life. He'd been ten at the time and what he remembered most was the smell of the place and the inhuman noises that issued from the unseen inmates. Sometimes he'd kick up a fuss and refuse to accompany his grandmother. More even than the anguish of missing his mother was the unbearable knowledge that, as they approached the wing that housed her, he'd look up and see her pale face at the window watching for them. One night she'd ended their combined misery by swallowing all the pills she'd hoarded, and the only thing he remembered feeling was relief. For years he'd buried the memory in the dark of his unconscious, until now when it broke free with all the force of neglect.

He sat down on a bench, struggling to regain his calm. They were in a long corridor that went all round the building, punctuated at intervals by staircases to the upper storeys. Everything bespoke misery, from the furrows in the parquet flooring, gouged out by the constant passage of shuffling feet, to the walls whose pastel colours were a feeble attempt to disguise the wretchedness. Even the statue of the leaping deer in the entrance hall seemed poised for the bullet that would strike it down, as if caught in the act of its own destruction. He couldn't bear to think of Isobel in this place of broken hearts.

Martha observed what she took to be his shock of realising the gravity of Isobel's situation.

'She's been moved to her own room. Her father's on the hospital board... At least that way she's still able to make her wonderful creations. I've never known anyone so inventive. Whatever materials she lays her hands on, she turns into something miraculous.'

Her attempt at offering reassurance did little to assuage his horror. He forced himself to stand upright and they set off again, climbing two flights of stairs to the top floor. He felt as if he were viewing things through the wrong end of a telescope and barely heard the attendant, who unlocked the door to the high security wing, remarking that the young lady was quiet today and in better form. They reached a door where Martha halted. She tapped and, without waiting for an answer, opened it.

The afternoon was drawing in yet the room was full of colour and muted light. A barred window overlooked the garden, through which gleams of winter sun mingled with the softer glow from the lamps. Shades of handmade paper threw coloured patterns onto the rug. In the centre of the room stood the loom he'd seen in Isobel's attic studio and on it a strip of luminous blue and green cloth, in the process of being woven. On the work table were piled drawings in pencil, charcoal and pastel and in the far corner was a harp. Isobel stood with her back to the window, silhouetted against the dying afternoon so that at first he could not make out her features. Martha went to her and took her hand.

'I've brought someone to see you. You remember Simon?'

'Simon... Oh, yes! '

She took a step forward, shifting from monochrome to colour, and held out her hand. As he took it he thought how unexpectedly dry her skin felt, like a snake.

'How did you find me?'

'Martha...'

"I mean my home address.'

'I found Grimalkin.'

'The cat? How is he? Surviving, no doubt. There's plenty of hunting up there.'

The casual way she referred to the pet she'd previously lavished with affection made him wonder if she actually remembered the creature. Martha fished out a white cardboard box from her shopping bag and set it on the table.

'I brought a cake. Shall I make tea?'

Isobel nodded and Martha carried the kettle into the adjacent bathroom.

She gestured him to sit down. Her regal manner seemed designed to hold him at arm's length. He longed to go to her and take her in his arms but, conscious of her vulnerability, knew he must not alarm her.

'It's a surprise to see you but a pleasant one. I don't get many visitors.'

She gave a brief laugh, almost a giggle.

'I guess they're afraid to come here.'

'It's not the best of places.'

He observed again how graceful she was, in a way that made everyone else seem gauche and clumsy.

Martha returned and they had tea. He spoke about his job and flat hunting, though he was aware how little these things interested Isobel. She listened politely and toyed with a few crumbs of cake. She was painfully thin yet there was nothing weak or feeble about her. He wanted to tell her that he understood how she wore her frailty as a disguise, a way to fool predators. He would have reassured her that never would he be found amongst their ranks. But instead he asked her about her work and at once her face lit up. The hospital had finally agreed to let her have materials - needles, thread and fabric for the puppets she intended to make. She and some of the other inmates had plans to put on a puppet show. He pointed to the harp and asked if she played. She replied that she was familiar with a few of the old airs but wanted to learn to play properly. She hoped to have lessons, if a teacher could be found.

'Perhaps if you come again, we can sing together. I'm sure you have a beautiful voice.'

For the first time she turned to him directly and he recognised in her strange blue gaze a look of pleading.

'I'd like that, though I'm not so sure about my voice.'

These days, he thought with shame, he did little more than earn money from a job that meant nothing to him. Once he'd fancied himself as a potter and had set up a kiln in the corner of a friend's studio. He realised, with all the force of revelation, how he longed to do something creative, and the irony of rediscovering that desire in this, of all places, was not lost on him. She, on the other hand, would let nothing deter her, even though he could see the cost that exacted in the tic that had started up in her cheek and the weariness gathered behind her eyes. Only by pushing herself to the limit and beyond could she prove her indestructibility and free herself from those who set out to restrain her. But how long could she hold out?

Martha, sensing danger, kept her gaze on Simon. She realised she had made a terrible mistake in inviting him to accompany her. What she had thought of as a genuine attachment and a way to cheer Isobel up, was in truth merely one more hunter's search for his prey. She had fought off other, more dangerous predators and knew well how all that was beautiful and rare about Isobel excited them. Ever since the child had been handed over to her, she had made it her mission in life to save her at any cost, including from those closest and most expected to protect her. But she had underestimated this young man. The girl had often talked of him as a soul mate and like a fool she'd believed her. Now she saw that whatever it was they shared, far from pulling her back from the abyss above which she teetered, he would tip her into it and himself after her.

She got up abruptly, announcing that it was time to go.

The young people made no move as if they hadn't heard her. She grabbed Simon by the arm and propelled him roughly to the door. He was surprised at her strength and barely took in Isobel's polite thanks for coming and her hope that he would return some day. Before he could gather himself, the door of her room closed firmly behind him and he found himself outside in the corridor.

Half way down the passage, he came to his senses. He wrenched himself free from the old woman's grasp and ran back to Isobel's door. He hammered on it, crying out that he understood as no one else could what it was like for her to be shut up in this place. He would liberate her... But as he formulated the words, his throat grew dry and he could make no sound.

An attendant ran up and grabbed hold of him. He strong-armed him to the staircase and Simon heard the security door clang to behind them. As they descended the stairs, he understood that the sobbing that filled his ears was his own and knew it was as much for himself as for Isobel. Through her he had seen an escape route out of the desert of meaninglessness that was his life. He had glimpsed salvation, only to be cast back into emptiness.

They were nearing the exit. Soon it would be too late and she'd be lost to him forever. He stopped in his tracks so that the man holding him stumbled and almost lost his footing. An idea had struck him, in which he discerned a ray of hope. Like the prisoner who is deprived of everything but the last trivial object in his possession, he clung to it for dear life.

The attendant asked if he was all right. He smiled reassuringly and they resumed their walk. He would give nothing away. Then, when the fuss had died down and they'd forgotten who he was, he would offer himself as the singing teacher Isobel sought and, like the vampire answering the call of his victim, he would return to her and suck her dry.

Circe

Mike Simons was a composer. After an acclaimed graduation piece scored for choir, full orchestra and four soloists, he was determined not to compromise his ambition to make his name and living from music. Between various jobs done purely to pay the rent, he'd written some songs for a couple of up and coming singers, done some arranging for various bands and rescored a musical for the stage, which still toured the regional theatres. Recently he had been commissioned to write the score for a feature length TV film about James Joyce. This, he reckoned, would be his big break.

His knowledge of Irish music was hazy. But there was an old song he'd once heard, accompanied by a harp, that never ceased to haunt him. It was in the unlikely setting of a London psychiatric hospital where he was working during the summer, hosting the in-house radio show whilst the usual guy was on holiday. One hot afternoon as he gazed out of the window at the shrivelled lawns and wilting flowerbeds of the hospital garden, the voice and liquid sound of the harp drifted down on the air to his makeshift studio, plangent and unbearably moving. It came from an upper storey where the long-term patients were housed and when he asked to meet the singer, he was told it wasn't possible. In compensation he'd opted for a recording by the Chieftains. But the rendering of that unknown harpist still echoed in his dreams.

Now he was off to Ireland to seek out the real music, in contrast to what could be heard in every Irish theme pub. Go west, he was told. So he flew to Dublin and made his way across country by bus, stopping off wherever the fancy took him. Most of what he heard was disappointing, commercial stuff played on electric guitars with a heavy rock base. He was beginning to think the Irish weren't interested any longer in the old ways of singing, accompanied only by a fiddle or a pipe.

* * *

A sudden hush fell over the company in Macfadden's bar as the stranger entered the room, causing Margaret to look up from the glasses she was washing. She saw a young man of around thirty, quite stocky, with close-cropped curly dark hair and eyes like shiny black coals. It was the man from her dream and the shock of seeing him standing before her was momentarily fazing. Two nights ago she had dreamt of him again and woke filled with dread. He looked foreign, Spanish or perhaps Maltese. They'd had two of those staying last summer. The weather had been terrible so they'd only stopped one night. But when he asked for a pint of Guinness, she noted his accent was pure English.

You could cut the silence with a knife. The old fools regarded strangers with a mixture of curiosity and resentment at the intrusion. Not that there were many strangers at this time of the year. The young man asked if it was possible to get something to eat. She said she'd some ham and could fry up a couple of eggs if that would do him and he thanked her and said it would do nicely. The way he looked at her, she could tell he thought her a striking woman. He took a seat at an empty table near the fire. It was a chilly evening, despite the warm September day, and he was glad of the fire. She retreated to the back kitchen and the men resumed their talk.

When the Guinness was ready one of the regulars, Colm Docherty, who'd taken Margaret's place behind the bar, brought it over. Mike was gazing up at the TV on the wall, which was showing a sports programme with the sound turned down so it was inaudible. Margaret had been forced to put up a TV for the sake of the regulars but she disliked it and only acceded as long as the sound was kept down. The exception was when a local team was playing.

'Is it Dublin you're from?' Colm inquired.

Mike nodded.

'I came by bus. It must have been the scenic route because it took hours.'

He reached out a hand, which Colm took in his gnarled one.

'Mike Simons.'

'Colm Docherty. Welcome to Kinadoohy. So what brings you to these parts? It's late now for visitors.'

'The music. I'm told you've the real stuff here.'

'You've come to the right place all right. None of your karaoke here. Just the old fiddlers and pipers.'

Margaret entered with a plate of food, which she set down on the table together with a knife and fork wrapped in a paper napkin.

'Margaret here has the voice of an angel. When she can be persuaded to sing, which is seldom enough these days.'

'There's no need to talk about me as if I weren't here and hadn't a tongue in me head.'

But Colm was not to be put off.

'A man from Dublin wanted to sign her up. He'd a big tour planned and everything but she wouldn't go.'

'Perhaps you'll give me the chance to hear you sometime.'

She felt the stranger's gaze on her but made no response.

Seamus O'Malley entered and Margaret disappeared into the back kitchen. He walked to the bar with the deliberate step of the habitual drunk and banged on the counter.

'Is there no one here to give a thirsty man a drink?'

He was a tall, handsome man, made gaunt by loneliness and drink. There was something shy, almost feral, about him which he attempted to mask by aggression. Colm went behind the bar to serve him.

'This is Mike, our young visitor from Dublin. He's here for the music.'

Seamus barely glanced at him.

'A long way to come for a tune.'

'I'm researching the music for a film on James Joyce. Your great writer.'

Seamus eyed the stranger. No doubt the young fool imagined no one here had ever heard of Joyce, though there were those present who'd read every word the fella ever wrote.

'That old fraud! Couldn't get out of Ireland quick enough then spent the rest of his life getting rich telling lies about it. What did he call this country? "An old sow that eats her farrow!"'

'His wife Norah was from these parts. A fine-looking woman by all accounts,' Colm intervened.

'So I believe. Joyce called her the Ireland he carried with him wherever he went.'

Seamus gave a snort of disgust.

'Not for sure the Ireland of those fighting and dying to defeat the tyranny back home.'

'Still you can't deny, Seamus, the man wrote some grand books.'

'And who reads them but foreigners and those like himself, hypocrites with an eye for smut.'

'You talk like some ignorant old ballocks of a priest,' Sean said, joining them.

'I'm not forgetting the betrayals of Mother Church either.'

'That's the trouble with this country. There's too much remembering altogether.'

'Can't you leave your blessed arguments for one night of the year!' Margaret declared, emerging from the back kitchen.

The men, including Seamus, fell silent as if by her command.

The pints continued to line up in front of Mike and at length the music began. Poraig Moynahan got out his fiddle and someone else beat out a rhythm on the bodhran. Sean sang an old song in Gaelic full of loss and exile with a passion that moved everyone, including Margaret. His face was smooth and rosy-cheeked like a baby, despite his sixty-odd years, and he stretched out his throat like a heron to emit a high, keening sound. Mike had never heard singing like it and, determined to miss nothing, he switched on the small recorder he took with him wherever he went.

When the song was finished, Sean took up a pipe and played a couple of rousing reels with the other musicians. By now Mike was struggling to keep his eyes open. He wasn't much of a drinker and he was exhausted after his long journey. Walking as steadily as he could, he went up to the bar.

'Have you a room free? I saw the B&B sign over the entrance.'

Margaret nodded and bade him follow her. She led the way through the door at the far end of the bar to a staircase. He noticed admiringly as she climbed the stairs the way she carried herself and the sway of her shapely hips. When they reached the landing, she opened the door to a simple room.

'There's no en suite and the toilet's down there in the yard. But there's clean sheets and I'll bring you up some hot water in the morning.'

He thanked her, trying to think of something to detain her but she was already gone. He collapsed fully clothed onto the bed and in a few minutes was asleep.

Margaret locked the doors behind the last of her customers, washed and put away the glasses then climbed the stairs for bed. She was tired but too restless to sleep. A full moon filled the room with its unearthly light and was reflected in the pier glass at the end of the bed. She stood in front of the mirror and loosed her hair, which in the moonlight was the colour of dried blood. The skin on her full breasts and on her belly and thighs gleamed white and translucent and she swayed her body gently as if to music. She was still a fine looking woman in her prime, despite having borne two children and passed her fortieth year. Men desired her and she could have her pick of the town if she wanted, married or not. But she wasn't interested. To one man only, the father of her children, she had given herself but that was long ago and she no longer mourned him. Now her son was grown and studying to become a doctor in Dublin even though she, his mother, could barely read or write. Occasionally she thought wistfully of the opportunities he'd had that hadn't been there for her as a girl, but not often. She was her own woman with few regrets.

There was one thing that troubled her, though, and with increasing force. She felt a growing restlessness, not for a man, though she had nothing against the pleasures of love, but a hunger to see something of the world. It started when her son returned from a vacation job with an international medical organisation. He had talked of the wonders he had seen and shown her photographs he'd taken. The stories he'd told had given birth to an intense longing to leave this place where she'd spent her whole life and to seek out new horizons before it was too late. After that she would be content to return and live out the rest of her days, indifferent to the town and its inhabitants who lacked all curiosity because they held themselves to be the finest specimens of the human race.

'Pigs,' she muttered, 'content to wallow in their own muck!'

The house was quiet. So quiet she could hear the stranger breathing in the next room. She remembered her dream of the previous night. She'd known he was coming for her, heard his approaching tread with a mixture of anticipation and dread, looking for somewhere to hide though it was already too late. Perhaps the dream had meant something after all and this man had come with a purpose. She'd heard mention of a job in TV, which suggested connections with money and influence. He might help her to find a job where she could earn what she needed to pay for her travels, which she had no chance of doing here. She'd be happy to clean the houses of the rich, cook, do laundry and make herself useful in a hundred different ways. She was nothing if not resourceful. Her head buzzed with ideas and plans, and it was a long time before she fell asleep.

The following morning was fine, the sky a pure, washed blue with a few fast-moving clouds blowing in from the west. Margaret began to sing as she hung out the washing in the yard. Her daughter Kathleen sat on the doorstep talking to her rag doll in a strange, whispery voice. Her mother had made the doll when she was four and although she was now almost thirteen, it still figured in the games she liked to play. She was a serious child, young for her age but good at her school work. Some people thought her not quite right in the head. She was so quiet and came out with such odd things. But Margaret knew there was nothing wrong that an education and getting away from this town wouldn't fix. At first she sang softly to herself but soon she forgot she might be overheard and allowed her voice free rein. She did not look up when a head emerged from the window above.

Mike peered down into the yard. It was her voice which had woken him from a deep sleep, insinuating itself into his dreams like smoke on the air and, before he was properly awake, he had reached for his recorder and stumbled to the window. He gazed down at the woman below pegging out the wet clothes on the line, at the shapely curve of her neck and strong uplifted arms that made her breasts strain at the bodice of her dress.

When she had finished, she picked up the basket and went back into the house. Mike sat down on his bed and reran the tape. Her voice stirred him like nothing had done since the harp player in the psychiatric hospital. Its effect was magnified by the image of bare, uplifted arms and sunlight on auburn hair. It seemed she had been singing for him, though she'd not been aware of his presence. This, he realised, was the inspiration he'd been seeking, the muse to inspire him to greatness. He wondered if there was a man or an absent lover. There was a child whom he presumed to be hers, a strange little thing with a head too big for her body. But so far he'd seen no sign of a husband.

The day was humid and the room felt stuffy. He needed to get out and clear his head. He found a jug of now tepid water outside his door, washed and dressed and without bothering about breakfast set out to walk across the bog.

As he picked his way over the uneven ground, the air was full of sounds that made music in his head. From time to time he paused to record the calling of birds or the wind as it sang through the telegraph wires and fence posts and the rasping of tree branches. The power to transform random dissonance to harmony through music filled him with a sense of boundless excitement.

When he returned Margaret was in the grocery store, which formed the other half of the ground floor of the house, divided from the bar by a central passage. She was unpacking a consignment of goods that had just been delivered and putting them into the freezer. She looked up as Mike entered the house, attempting to slip down the passage unnoticed. His jeans were covered in mud and his teeshirt green with slime. He looked so bedraggled it was all she could do not to burst out laughing.

'Jesus, Mary and Joseph! Whatever happened to you?'

He paused reluctantly.

'I went for a walk and fell in the bog. At least my tape recorder survived.'

He held it up as if in some way it justified the rest of his appearance.

'You'd best get out of them wet clothes. You'll catch your death.'

'I've only these jeans. Stupid, I know. Travelling light!'

She shut the lid of the freezer and came out into the passage.

'Then we'll find you something to wear.'

'Thanks, but they'll dry in no time.'

She moved past him, heading for the back kitchen, opened the door and gestured him in. He had little choice but to obey.

It was a low-ceilinged room, warm and comfortably furnished with an old-fashioned range that served for cooking and heating the water, a table and two armchairs over which a pair of brightly coloured, hand-crocheted blankets had been thrown. A peat fire burned in the hearth and there were children's paintings pinned to the wall, luridly coloured scenes of rocks and shipwrecks with tiny figures leaping from pitching decks into the foaming water. Kathleen was seated at the table, drawing. She drew with remarkable fluency, making swift stabbing motions at the paper with her pencil.

'Fetch me a basin of hot water, girl, and be quick about it,' Margaret ordered and turned to Mike, who still hung in the doorway.

'Come over to the fire and take off them wet things.'

He peeled off his socks and teeshirt in as casual a manner as possible, whilst she rummaged in the press that stood in the corner of the room and brought out a pair of much washed cord trousers, a shirt, sweater and pair of thick woollen socks. He looked down and saw the mud that oozed stickily between his toes and left footprints on the scrubbed floor. Kathleen set down a basin of hot water next to him, stifling a giggle. The glance of merriment that passed between mother and daughter added to his humiliation. They were enjoying seeing him stripped virtually naked. Margaret handed him a towel and placed the clothes on a chair.

'Take these and give me yours. I'll have them washed and dried for you in no time.'

He handed her his socks and teeshirt.

'And the rest. I doubt you've anything I've not seen before.'

Neither she nor her monster of a daughter could restrain their laughter as he peeled off his jeans but he wasn't going to give them the satisfaction of his nakedness. Holding tight to his boxers, he grabbed the clothes and almost ran from the room as sounds of merriment pursued him up the stairs.

In his room he put on the borrowed garments. They were the kind of clothes an elderly uncle who fancied himself a bit of a country gent would have gone in for. They made him look like a scarecrow. The wind had got up and it had grown quite chilly so he was forced to wear them but he wasn't going to parade himself before the village. He spent the afternoon listening to the sounds he'd recorded and trying them out in various combinations. At around six there was a tap on the door. Kathleen handed him his clothes, ironed and neatly folded, together with a hot cup of tea and a couple of biscuits in the saucer. He thanked her perfunctorily and wolfed down the biscuits. He hadn't eaten all day. An hour later he was down in the bar.

The musicians had already arrived and were warming up. Sean sang in his strange keening voice and someone else followed with a couple of rebel songs. No one paid much attention to Mike, seated at his table with his recorder switched on beside him. Kathleen brought him a plate of mackerel with boiled potatoes and cabbage, which hungry as he was he thought the most delicious food he'd ever tasted. Colm was doing duty behind the bar and though Mike was on the alert for the appearance of Margaret, there was no sign of her.

Increasingly restless, he turned down the continuous offers of pints as graciously as he could and was finding it hard to concentrate on the music. Eventually, feeling slightly feverish from his adventure on the bog, he decided to get an early night. Upstairs he lay in his bed, hearing the voices below that mingled with the wind in the trees and the occasional hoot of an owl. It reminded him of when he was a child, listening to the talk and laughter of the adults downstairs, and half-resenting his exile. But soon he was asleep, dreaming of an unknown woman whom he knew was Margaret.

The following morning he awoke refreshed and full of energy. He got up, washed, dressed, and went downstairs. There was no sign of anyone in the bar or shop so he knocked on the door of the back kitchen. Margaret opened it. She was dressed in jeans and a frayed baggy sweater and her hair hung down over her shoulders. She looked beautiful.

'You're up early. Breakfast'll be a few minutes.'

He smiled.

'No rush. Thanks for my clothes. Ironed too! I don't deserve it.'

She didn't respond but seemed not displeased by his gratitude.

'I'll bring your breakfast to the bar.'

He hovered in the doorway.

'Actually I wanted to ask you something. Will you come for a walk with me?'

'A walk?'

She looked astonished.

'Haven't you enough of walking after your escapade on the bog.'

'I thought we could go to the beach.'

'It's just a strand like any other.'

He waited, willing her to accept.

'What about your breakfast?'

'Later.'

'I can't just drop everything.'

'Why not?'

She hesitated then went over to the mirror above the hearth. She ran her fingers through her hair.

'Your hair's lovely like that.'

She turned back to him.

'Pass me my jacket then.'

He took the jacket from the peg behind the door and handed it to her with a little bow.

'Thank you, kind sir,' she replied coquettishly.

She took off the baggy sweater, put on the jacket and wound a bright scarf about her head to keep back her hair.

'How do I look?'

'A picture for sore eyes!'

She laughed.

'We'd better go out the back way. To avoid the prying eyes.'

As they walked up the village street side by side their hands brushed against each other, sending a frisson of desire through his body.

Just before they reached the turn off to the shore, they ran into Sean with his donkey and a huge load of seaweed.

'Off on your travels? You've a grand day for it!'

'We have indeed,' Mike returned cheerfully.

Margaret said nothing until Sean was out of earshot.

'It'll be all over town by this afternoon. The two of us out walking together.'

'So?'

'You don't know this place!'

The bitterness of her tone took him by surprise.

The path ran down to a small quay, from where the shore opened out into a sandy bay ending in a tangle of rocks and towering cliffs. The day was fine but the wind was getting up and whenever the sun went behind a cloud, it felt quite chilly. A couple of boats were tied up at the quayside but the strand itself was deserted.

They set off in the direction of the cliffs. Mike tried to think of something to break the silence, though the buffeting wind made it hard to talk. Margaret seemed to have withdrawn into herself. He glanced down at the sand and pointed to the trail of footprints spreading out behind them.

'Look! Our traces.'

'The tide will soon wash them away.'

She seemed distant but nothing could dampen his spirits. Everything about this place and, above all, being here with her, filled him with joy.

'You're not sorry you came?'

Her reply was carried off by the blast.

'Let's find somewhere out of the wind.'

'I shouldn't have come.'

He reached for her hand and together they ran towards the rocks, scrambling over them until they reached the great overhang of cliff where the wind suddenly calmed. They leaned their backs against its fissured surface and gazed out to sea. He kept hold of her hand and she made no attempt to draw it away.

'Tell me you're not sorry you came.'

She shook her head.

'You've got an amazing voice. What stopped you singing?'

She paused for a moment, as if deciding whether or not to speak.

'The boy I was going to Dublin with took off without me and my Da forbade me to follow. I was 17.'

'But later? You must have had other opportunities.'

'He left me pregnant and I'd no money and nowhere else to go. My Ma was dead and my brothers gone abroad for the work so there was only me to look after my Da. I kept the house for him but he gave me no money, not that he'd any to give. He was never much of a provider.'

'And the baby?'

'I lost it in the third month. Many times I thought of leaving but I didn't know how. Then one day the priest came to me. He'd heard of my misfortune and knew a man in a town a few miles off. A good man, he said, who was looking for a wife. He worked at the fishing, salmon in summer and shark in winter. He'd a house and a couple of acres, decent land where you could grow vegetables. He knew my story and said it didn't bother him. At first I wouldn't listen but in the end I agreed to meet him. Da was drinking and our bit of a farm was gone to rack and ruin so what did I have to lose?'

'So you married.'

'Ten years we had together. It was true what the priest said. He was a good man and loved me as much as any man could.'

'What happened to him?'

'He drowned. The sea can be treacherous even to those who know it well and the shark swim far out. They never found the boat nor the body.'

Growing up in a suburb of south London, Mike could scarcely imagine a life such as hers. Her hair had come loose from the scarf and blew about her face in wild tendrils and her eyes had taken on the same greenish hue as the sea.

'I've never met a woman like you, Margaret.'

He took off his coat and laid it on the cold sand then reached out for her and drew her down without resistance. At first his caresses were tentative and uncertain but her responsiveness drew him on, until he knew nothing but the saltiness of her kisses and the warmth of her body which received him with an abandon he had never before experienced.

Afterwards she sat up, propping herself on one elbow to gaze at him. He smiled at her in a trance of happiness.

'Will you do something for me?'

'Name it.'

'I have to see the world before I die.'

'Then you must start singing again. With your voice you could go anywhere. It's not too late.'

The idea that he might be her Svengali, use his contacts to launch her career, fired him with excitement.

'It is for me.'

'I'm not saying it'd be easy. But nowadays with modern technology you could start right here. I can help you.'

'That's not what I want.'

But his thoughts were running away with him.

'The first thing is to record something, put a song out on the internet to generate interest. Then we can go to a producer.'

'I'd be no good at that. Besides I want to go where I want, be who I want, not be told what to do by producers or managers.'

He looked at her, trying to understand.

'If I went to London, it'd not be hard to find me a job.'

'In a club? London's a pretty tough place to start out.'

'I mean in London I'd be able to earn money, which I can never do here. It wouldn't have to be singing.'

'What else then?'

'A housekeeper or a cleaner, a childminder, anything! You must know people. You could ask them for me.'

She had lost him.

'You want to be a cleaner?'

'I don't care. As long as I can earn money.'

It was only to be expected, he thought. She'd lost confidence in herself, stuck here all her life with no one to encourage her. But he would rekindle that faith and turn her into the great artist she was destined to be.

'Going to London's not the right thing just now. You've got to trust me on this.'

She buttoned up her jacket and stood up.

'We'd better go back. We'll be cut off by the tide.'

'Wait, Margaret. I ... '

He reached out for her but she was gone, hurrying away over the rocks. He scrambled up and tried to follow but slipped and jammed his foot between boulders, twisting his ankle painfully. It wasn't until he'd regained the sands that he finally caught up with her. Hobbling beside her, he tried to find something soothing to say. He knew he'd ruined what had gone before, though he didn't really know why. It was as if she had thrown a wall up around herself, impossible to penetrate.

The sun was sinking and the outgoing tide left a scum of debris - bladderwrack, bits of old rope, cartons and plastic bottles. As they neared the end of the strand, a boat rounded the headland making for the quay. Margaret halted.

'You go on. Don't wait for me.'

'But I ...'

'Please, do as I say!'

Without another glance, she turned away and headed down towards the quay.

Up in his room, Mike went over the events of the afternoon. Sexual gratification had given way to self-recrimination, though for the life of him he couldn't say what exactly had gone wrong. Margaret's request to find her a job, any job in London made no sense to him. Unless it was that she was not the free woman she appeared to be and was merely using him to make her escape. The more he considered it, her surrender on the beach had been almost too easy. He had been lulled into imagining himself the seducer, when in fact he was the seduced. He'd thought there was something more between them than just sexual desire - a shared passion for music. Now he wondered whether, apart from her great gift, she was no different from the rest of these people whose principal satisfaction seemed to be making a fool out of any unsuspecting outsider who came their way.

He came down to the bar in sullen mood. Seamus O'Malley was already there, goading Sean with a malevolence he passed off as humour.

'She'll have you tarred and feathered if that field's not done by Friday.'

'I'm telling you, that woman thinks more of her old field than she does of her own son. Why, she'd have the devil himself on all fours and him thanking her for the work.'

Seamus laughed.

'Now, man, that's no way to speak of your old mammy.'

Mike caught the malicious gleam in his eye as he turned in his direction.

'Well, if it isn't our young visitor! I hear you've been taking a ducking yourself.'

'The bog's a treacherous place,' Sean said.

'No more than anywhere else around here.'

Seamus ignored the innuendo.

'How's the Joyce coming along?'

'Fine.'

He had no desire to point out it was the music not Joyce that concerned him.

'Aye, the dead make grand companions. They seldom argue!'

'Did you enjoy your walk this afternoon?' Sean said.

'Yes, thanks.'

'The tide comes in pretty quick round them cliffs. You need to take care.'

He wondered for a moment if they'd observed him and Margaret together under the cliff. It mattered little to him, though it would be awkward for Margaret.

'One thing about your Joyce fella people around here could never understand,' Seamus went on.

'Oh? What was that?'

'His not fighting for his woman. Oh, she stuck to him all right. But in the end, she told her sister, he wasn't a true man.'

So that was it. Seamus had designs on Margaret, though it was scarcely possible she reciprocated his feelings. Mike felt a brief sense of triumph over such a doomed rival.

They were interrupted by Kathleen to ask if ham and eggs would do for his supper.

'And tell Margaret while she's about it, Seamus'ld not say no to a bit of that salmon I caught for her today.'

'My orders are to look after our guest here, not fetch and carry for the likes of you,' Kathleen retorted and turned on her heel.

Seamus went over to join the men, who'd begun filtering in for the evening's drinking, and Mike took a seat at his usual table. His bad mood was not improved by his spat with Seamus and he ate his supper without relish. He longed for a glimpse of Margaret and had almost given up hope, when he looked up and there she was.

She was wearing a blue dress of some soft silky material, which showed off her figure, and had arranged her hair so that it loosely framed her face. She looked astonishingly beautiful and all his suspicions evaporated as he gazed at her, full of admiration and desire. Tucking a stray lock behind her ear, she stepped out from behind the bar.

'Poraig, d'you recall "The Lass of Aughrim"?'

The room fell silent. All eyes were on her. Poraig ran through the opening bars on his fiddle and the other musicians joined in, running with the tune. For a moment the room held its breath then Margaret began to sing. Her pure voice wove in and out of the instruments, breathing life into the passionate words of the song so that they penetrated the heart of each listener with their grief and longing.

At length it was over and there was silence. Then the company burst into applause and people began shouting and stamping their feet for more. She shook her head and went back behind the bar. But the clamour kept up, Mike being among the loudest. When her indifference made it clear she would sing no more, people eventually returned to their talk and their drinking.

Alone at his table, Mike checked his tape recorder to make sure he'd missed none of her performance. He was drinking far more than he usually did but it seemed only to increase his feelings of frustration. Irritated by the mundane conversations of the men, he observed Margaret as she came and went behind the bar, serving her customers with a natural grace that held everyone at bay. Several times he went up to renew his glass in the hope of a brief touch of her hand or the flash of a smile, but he received nothing.

He'd lost count of the pints he'd consumed when Seamus O'Malley rose unsteadily to his feet.

'I'll give you a song. "Moses O'Toural ai ay".'

Mike knew his words were directed at him.

'Sing what you bloody well like. It's your sodding country,' he growled.

But Seamus wasn't finished.

'And we'll thank you to remember it. This one's not to show the love between the Irish and the Jewish people but the stupidity of the English.'

He'd had enough. If Seamus wanted a fight, he'd get one. He rose to his feet. But at that moment he felt his stomach cramp and his gorge rise and only just made it across the bar and out into the yard. As the night air clutched his beer-bloated belly, he bent over and vomited profusely. Afterwards he leaned his back against the wall, raising his saliva-streaked face to the sky. The stench of vomit filled his nostrils but he felt calmer. All he wanted was to lie down in the comforting privacy of his room. Perhaps in a moment or two he could make it back inside and up the stairs without anyone noticing.

The back door opened, illuminating him in a shaft of light. He blinked in the sudden brightness. The next moment his head slammed back against the wall and a voice in his ear hissed, 'Go home, English bastard!' An unprecedented rage seized hold of him. He brought his knee up sharply and, with a thrill of pleasure, felt the softness of the other man's groin crush against the blow and heard his groan. Two hands went round his throat and work-thickened fingers pressed the arteries on either side of his neck, until his eyes bulged and he thought he was going to choke. From somewhere in his distant past he heard his father shout, 'If you can't fight fair, lad, fight dirty!' Wriggling his arms free from the wall where they were pinned by the other man's weight, he shoved his fingers as hard as he could into the man's eyeballs. With a shout of pain Seamus let go, whereupon Mike collapsed to his knees, cracking his forehead on the ground.

There were voices and a woman's shouting. He was dimly aware of being lifted and carried back into the house. Margaret's face floated above him and, despite the pain in his head and a bloody lip, he did his best to smile. Then he was lying on his bed and the walls of his room were pitching round him like a tossing ship. He leaned over and was sick into a basin someone had left there, and after that he slept.

Margaret lay staring up at the ceiling, naked in a pool of moonlight. It was not so much the brightness as rage that kept her awake. Mike, with his handsome looks and fine education, was no different from the rest of the swine that surrounded her, before whom she had long since declined to scatter the pearls of her gift. But tonight she had sung for him, and instead of receiving that as the gift it was, he'd got falling-down drunk out of pique at her refusal to see him as the conquering hero. He had no idea what her voice meant to her, a blessing to be bestowed when and how she wished, not sold to the highest bidder. She understood now the dread that had accompanied her dream of his coming. If this man were to be the harbinger of her fate, she would need to protect herself.

The following morning she was opening up the bar, when Seamus slunk in. She knew from his hangdog appearance and the earliness of the hour that he had something on his mind.

'I'm sorry, Margaret, for last night's disturbance.'

'You know my feelings about people bringing their private quarrels into my house.'

'I do, and I admit things got out of hand. But the fella had it coming.'

'That makes little difference.'

He hesitated. It was clear he had more to say.

'Why did you sing for him?'

'Who says it was for him?'

'You never sing these days and I know it was.'

He hesitated again.

'D'you want him taking care of?'

She held his eye.

'What you do off my premises is your own business, Seamus O'Malley. Now, take yourself off. I've work to do.'

She saw his gaze brighten and knew he received her words as permission to teach the young fool a lesson he wouldn't forget. She sighed but said nothing, and Seamus left the bar.

It was almost midday when Mike awoke to the sound of a donkey braying. He lay there listening and groaned inwardly to think what an ass he'd made of himself the previous night. His first instinct was to pack his bag and get out of there on the next bus. But he was damned if he'd be driven out like a beaten dog. He sat up and drank some water then picked up his tape recorder from the floor and pressed play. Margaret's voice rang out in all its bewitching purity. There was enough here to interest a recording agent, someone who could recognise a rare and striking talent, and he knew just the one. When he returned with a contract and the promise of enough money to go wherever she wanted, no strings attached, surely she could not fail to be gratified.

He got up, poured the jug of water over his head and neck, dried himself and put on his last clean teeshirt. He looked at himself in the cracked mirror above the washstand. There were dark bruises on either side of his neck and an egg on his forehead where he'd fallen, but apart from that he didn't look too bad.

Downstairs the bar was empty so he went to the kitchen door and knocked lightly. Kathleen opened it.

'Your breakfast'll be a few minutes,' she said and shut it again.

He took his seat in the bar to wait.

To his surprise it was Margaret who brought it to him.

'Sorry for all the bother last night,' he said as she set the plate down in front of him. 'I've made a firm resolution to stay off the drink in future.'

'You can't hold it, that's for sure.'

'I made an ass of myself. But I still mean it about helping you to become a singer.'

Her gaze fell to his mini recorder lying on the table next to his plate and her eyes blazed with sudden rage.

'You've my voice recorded on that thing? You're planning to sell my gift, which is mine and mine alone?'

'No! I made the recording so it won't be lost.'

'It was you I sang for not some agent fella. I'll see you in hell first!'

She picked up the recorder and, as Mike watched in horror, hurled it into the fireplace where it landed with a crack, and turned on her heel. He heard the kitchen door slam shut behind her. He wanted to go after her and tell her how unreasonable she was being, but he lacked the courage. Why had she sung for him if not to display her talent? And what possible reason had he given her to think he was out to exploit her, when he'd made it clear all along all he wanted was to give her the chance she deserved. The only thing left was to catch the next bus out of there and leave this accursed place behind.

He left his breakfast and went upstairs to pack his things. When he came down to settle up what he owed,

Margaret was nowhere to be seen. He found Kathleen in the yard, who told him her mother had gone down to the quay to pick up a consignment of fish.

As he turned into the road that led to the strand, he was met by a gust of strong wind. The sky had darkened and there was probably a storm out to sea. Reaching the quay, he saw Seamus emerging from one of the boats but no sign of Margaret. He was about to turn back but Seamus had already seen him.

'If it's Margaret you're after, you just missed her.'

'I need to pay her what I owe. I'm leaving on the next bus.'

'That calls for a wee drink.'

Seamus held out a half empty bottle of Paddy's.

'Let bygones be bygones and show there's no hard feelings.'

'Thanks. It's a bit early for me.'

'A cup of tea then, if that's more to your taste.'

He wanted nothing more than to tell the old fella to go fuck himself but at the same time he didn't want to leave on a bitter note.

'A quick one then. I don't want to miss the bus.'

'We'll make sure of that. Watch yourself now. The sea's choppy.'

He held the gangplank steady as Mike took hold of the pitching rail and heaved himself up. The boat stank of fish and diesel, which turned his stomach still delicate after last night's excess. He'd always hated boats and the sea made him sick at the best of times. He had to bow his head to enter the cramped cabin.

Seamus poured water from the kettle into a cup, added a teabag, milk and a large spoon of sugar and handed it to him. Mike glanced around him. Despite being crammed from floor to ceiling, the place had its own kind of orderliness and was no doubt the nearest thing Seamus had to a home. He was aware of the gaze fixed on him.

'Did you find what you came looking for?'

'I heard some fine music.'

'And Margaret? What did you think of her?'

'She's got a remarkable voice.'

'It's not all that's remarkable about her.'

'All that concerns me.'

Seamus's ravaged face creased into a grin.

'You're a fine liar, Mr Simons. Pity you fool no one.'

Mike felt a flicker of alarm as Seamus got up. He glanced out of the cabin window. The shore appeared to be drifting away. Then he heard the sound of the boat's engines being fired up and turned to see Seamus at the tiller. The boat leapt into motion and in no time they were bouncing across the waves and out to sea. He stumbled to the cabin door, grabbing the frame for support and cursing himself for the blind fool that he was.

Standing under the cliff, Margaret watched the boat dancing away over the grey water in a sudden burst of sunlight. She was not responsible for Mike's well being yet her heart was bleak. The blind self-centredness of men filled her with despair. If, even at this late hour,

Mike had asked her what it was she wanted and had listened to her answer, she would have forgiven him. Now he must take the consequences. Physically he was no match for Seamus, advanced in years as he was. But physical strength wasn't everything, as the heroes of old proved. Guile, rather than brute force, was what had enabled Ulysses to escape unharmed from the scrapes he found himself in, though Mike, she suspected, possessed little of that. In any case it was too late to help him now. Whatever power she had over her small realm, it was not superhuman.

She watched the boat until it disappeared around one of the islands, then left her shelter under the cliff and walked back along the strand. The sun was completely obscured by clouds. The days were drawing in and winter was coming. Once more the town would close in on itself with scarcely a stranger visiting. The winter months with her son gone made the daily routine more oppressive than ever. Many times she thought of just upping and leaving, despite having no money and nowhere to go. But it was too late. Here she could at least provide for Kathleen whose future, she feared, was bleak.

At the end of the evening, she tidied up the bar and went up to her room. She stood at the window, gazing out into the darkness. The sky was clearing again and the moon came and went behind slivers of cloud. In the distance a silver triangle of sea glistened beyond the dark shifting masses of trees and beneath her window the yard was full of shadows. They danced and trembled in the night wind. As she watched one detached itself from the rest, moving stealthily towards the house. She tensed but did not move as she heard a gentle knock on the door. It came again, more insistent. She put on her coat over her nightdress and went downstairs, quietly, so as not to disturb Kathleen.

She stood at the door, listening. She felt neither fear nor hope concerning the identity of whoever came knocking so late. It would be as it would be. A voice called out softly to open up. She hesitated a moment longer then drew back the bolt and opened the door. It was Mike who stood there on the threshold, drenched and shivering.

'You make a habit of appearing at my door like a drowned rat!' she said, holding it wider.

Inside the kitchen she motioned him to the fire and went to fill the kettle. He drew up a chair and sat holding out his hands to the glowing turves as small puddles gathered around his feet from his dripping clothes.

'Water! I hate the bloody stuff.'

His teeth were chattering.

'How did you get back to shore?'

'Swam.'

'And Seamus?'

'He fell asleep, eventually. The tide brought us in.'

He did not see the smile that flickered over her lips as she picked up the kettle to fill the teapot.

The heat from the turves began to seep into him and he could scarcely keep his eyes open. Yet his mind was clear as a bell. She poured a slug of whiskey into his tea and handed it to him.

'Was he drunk?'

'That, and lulled into unconsciousness by my talk! I told him my whole life story, until finally he could keep his eyes open no longer. It was the only way I could think of to distract him.'

'You're either a good liar or a lucky man.'

'Whichever it is, I made it back!'

He took a swig of his tea, feeling the warmth slide down his throat into his belly, whilst she stood there observing him. He had nearly drowned but at least he'd got the better of Seamus.

'You'll be needing your bed.'

'First I owe you an apology, Margaret.'

'For what exactly?'

She felt a faint stirring of hope.

'For turning, I suppose, into another of your swine.'

She let out a hoot of laughter.

'Well,' she said, observing him critically, 'swine can be turned back into men.'

Wolf Cubs

As the previous occupants rose to leave, Robby grabbed a couple of armchairs in the airport lounge coffee shop and flopped down. He stowed the hand luggage under the table and reached into his backpack for his inhaler. The place was bedlam and it was hard to find oxygen in the continuously recycled air. He searched for his Iplayer and plugged in the earphones. Music, he'd discovered, was the best way to get control over his breathing in panicky situations. Within seconds he felt his body begin to relax and fear of possible suffocation loosen its hold.

He was listening to an Irish singer he'd recorded under the table in a remote village somewhere in the west of Ireland, where he and his girlfriend Rosheen had stayed the previous summer. The singer's voice was remarkable and he'd played the song so much he'd had to ration himself for fear of wearing the thing out. He'd searched the internet but could find no recordings or even any reference to her. One day he planned to go back.

He and Rosheen were on their way to Canada for his brother's wedding. He hadn't seen his brother in over twenty years and had only decided on the visit after Rosheen had persuaded him this was a good moment, and if they didn't go now it'd be another twenty before they met. He saw her approaching with a tray of coffee and croissants. The sight of her never failed to evoke a quick surge of delight. With eyes more amber than hazel and red-gold curls that reminded him somehow of a dandelion clock, she was undeniably a beauty. But mostly there was something about her he never tired of and at the same time found impossible to put into words. He waved to signal his position.

'Large cappuccino for me, single macchiato for you.' She peered at him. 'You OK?'

'I will be as soon as we get moving. It's the waiting around that does it.'

They drank their coffee then set off on the fifteen minute walk to their gate. His mind was preoccupied with thoughts of his brother and he had to admit he wasn't looking forward to this visit. He and Rich were twins, separated at the age of eight by warring parents. Rich had remained in Canada with their father whilst their mother had taken him back to England, where she found work as a schoolteacher in Derby and eventually a new husband. At first he'd missed his brother desperately and even now he sometimes felt a nameless ache, as though a wound had never healed.

For several years they'd exchanged letters covered in drawings in the style of the comics that obsessed them both. They shared a facility for drawing, which soon became their principal means of communication. Then, for their fourteenth birthday, instead of the usual cartoon Robby received a photo of Rich. He was standing on some wild mountainside next to their father, both of them wearing identical red checked shirts, baseball caps and carrying hunting rifles. Robby held the picture against his own face, to compare their two reflections in the bathroom mirror in the house he shared with his mother and stepfather. The image of the manly youth in the photo spoke of a life full of adventure, whereas his own reflection showed a typical English schoolboy, hair parted, school tie and blazer, grey flannels with black, school-regulation lace-ups, and the nearest he got to the wild was walking the dog in the local park. He could still see the skinny boy that was his brother, leaping fearlessly from the rock that towered above the mosquito-infested creek where they swam in summer. His body made a perfect arc as it cleaved the water, clean as an arrow. Not to be outdone, Robby had shut his eyes, held his nose and, swallowing the ball of terror in his throat, with an incredible feat of will, launched himself feet first into the terrifyingly empty air.

He had few memories of Canada and most of them were of the outdoors, though with the long winters they must have spent much of their time inside. He remembered playing basketball with some of the neighbour kids in the yard, where their father had attached a net to one of the garage doors. Their father had also constructed a go-cart out of driftwood and old pram wheels on which they careered around the streets, mounting pavements and hurtling across junctions at peril of their lives. It made them the envy of the other kids. But one day they quarrelled over it so badly, he took the cart away and by the time he returned it they'd lost interest. It ended up on the Halloween bonfire.

Robby had few memories of his parents together and realised now his mother must have been depressed for a long time before they left. He could remember how, when he was small, he would lie in her lap and she would give him her secret smile that was for him alone. Her long hair fell down over her face to enclose the two of them in a soft curtain that shut out the rest of the world. Then one night he woke from a bad dream and went downstairs in his pyjamas. He could hear raised voices and as he watched through the crack in the door, he saw her crashing round the room, knocking into furniture like a blind person, whilst his father begged her to stay calm.

'Sybil! Please, my love!'

'You lied to me! Four days they were gone! Four days! Who knows what horrors they endured!'

Shortly before their ninth birthday their father announced that the Forestry Commission for whom he worked was sending him up north. It was the chance their mother had been waiting for. She declared that being in Canada was bad enough. But to go and live in some god-forsaken wilderness, with nothing but a bunch of inbreds and wild animals for company, would be the end of her.

Robby never saw his father again. For a while they exchanged postcards and talked on the phone at birthdays and Christmas. But the talks became increasingly awkward as they had less and less to say to each other and he came to dread them. Then five years ago his father died suddenly of a heart attack and, not long after, his mother succumbed to cancer.

His death was a shock since he was a fitness fanatic who'd lived most of his life out of doors. In contrast, hers was long and painful. Robby visited her in hospital as often as he could, but not enough to crush the pangs of guilt. He and Rosheen had just got together and it was hard, being newly in love, to have to spend so much of his free time at his mother's bedside. Rosheen proved more understanding than he could have imagined and the experience had cemented their relationship when it might easily have undermined it. He doubted, had the situation been the other way around, that he'd have been as patient and understanding.

On the plane they were served a meal on a plastic tray with some indifferent wine. Then the lights were dimmed and people settled down for the long haul. Most of the passengers, including Rosheen, put on blindfolds and earplugs and wrapped themselves in their blankets for the night. Robby followed suit but sleep evaded him. He searched for his Iplayer but realised it was inside the bag he'd stuffed into an upper locker and couldn't be reached without disturbing the rest of the row.

Journeying west meant it never grew properly dark and with his legs jammed up into the seat in front he was growing increasingly desperate. He swallowed a couple of pills, though he wasn't supposed to mix them with his inhaler, and put on his eye mask. He was beginning to feel a prickling sensation in his head like pins and needles, as he imagined the plane hurtling towards the edge of the world where it would pitch over and dive down, twisting and turning in a bottomless spiral. He sat up, took off the mask and tried watching the movie but quickly realised he'd seen it before and hadn't enjoyed it the first time.

By now most of the passengers had sunk into their own private dreams and the heat off so many breathing bodies was making him itch. The subliminal cacophony of sound that leaked from the headphones of non-sleepers invaded his scull and increased his desperation. He glanced down at Rosheen. She had stretched out across her own and the neighbour seat, which happened to be vacant, and was peacefully oblivious. He'd always admired her ability to adapt herself to any situation without complaint but he could stand it no longer. He extricated himself painstakingly and made his way down the gangway.

The rear portion of the aircraft was quiet, except for the throbbing of the engines, and there was room to move around. The cabin staff had retreated to wherever they could lie down undisturbed and it took him a moment to realise he was not alone. A woman stood with her back to him, gazing out of the uncurtained porthole. She turned briefly and nodded a greeting. He found her anonymous presence, like the throb of the engines, unexpectedly reassuring.

He took a step closer and saw over her shoulder, through the oval of glass, the evening endlessly reverse itself as the plane travelled westwards. The trail of a distant aircraft streaked across the space of livid sky, then dissipated and grew fainter before evaporating altogether. When he closed his eyes the imprint of its brightness remained, a luminous path into the void.

His eyeballs stung and he longed for darkness, some respite from the relentless day. But darkness also meant extinction. All his life he'd been afraid of that moment when he would cease to be, when he would dissolve like that exhaust trail and, with no record of his passing, leave behind not a trace.

The woman moved aside and Robby stretched out his hand to the window. The glass felt icy cold to his touch and his fingers left an imprint that lingered a moment before fading too. The fear that threatened to strangle his breathing moved to his stomach and a sudden nausea forced him to take refuge in the toilet. As he straightened up from the bowl and reached for paper to wipe his mouth, it occurred to him with a sense of shame that the woman outside might have heard sounds of his retching. He ran the tap for a long time, even after he'd washed his hands and rinsed out his mouth. His face when he looked in the mirror seemed to belong to a stranger.

A tapping on the door and the woman's voice roused him. He ran his fingers through his hair and unlocked the door.

'You OK?'

He nodded.

'Must be something I ate.'

'Probably. Airplane food's poison. I never touch it.'

She stepped closer and handed him a bottle of water.

'Take some of this.'

Her voice was foreign, Spanish, he thought. He took a long swig from the bottle and handed it back to her.

'Keep it.'

He looked closely at her for the first time. Her black hair was pulled back from a handsome face with strong brows separated by a fine down. Her eyes were amber flecked with yellow, and when they rested on him they seemed to penetrate to his very core. She was wearing a smart business suit that constricted her body like a slightly too tight skin, as if scarcely able to contain the vitality within. She seemed to emit an electrical force field, in which he too was held, and as she took a step closer, he felt her hot breath on his cheek.

'Here, let me.'

She brought out a linen handkerchief that smelt of cedar wood and wiped his wet face.

'Having a bit of a rough time?'

He seized her hand, smooth as a kid glove, and drew her close.

'Not here!'

She turned and led him to the far corner of the cabin where the light was dimmest. For a moment the musky scent of her body threatened to revive his nausea but his need for her was too great. He pressed himself against her, as he undid the buttons of her jacket and eased it off her shoulders. His hands strayed over the blue silk of her camisole and slipped down the straps to expose her breasts. He gazed in wonder at the pale, faintly freckled skin, tender and soft to his touch. She closed her eyes as his mouth fastened greedily onto her brown nipple.

'For a man who can't sleep on planes, you've been out for the count!'

Rosheen bent over him, fresh from a wash and brush up. He came to with a sense of bewilderment, not knowing where he was, and ran his fingers through his matted hair. His mouth felt parched and there was a dull throbbing in his temples.

'What time is it?'

'Time for a good dinner and a bottle of decent wine. We'll be there in fifteen minutes.'

She leaned over to kiss him but he turned his face aside.

'I need a wash first. I must smell like a skunk.'

Avoiding her eye, he got up and went to the toilet at the front of the plane. A feeling of shame dogged him, though he couldn't say why. Something to do with a dream, he felt sure it was a dream. He remembered a dark haired woman with amber eyes, and a feeling of nausea.

Rich was waiting in the arrivals lounge of Calgary airport. As the time for the plane's touchdown drew near, he wondered what crazy impulse had made him invite his brother over after so long a separation. A moment of sentimentality or some half-baked desire to draw a line under the past by confronting his ghosts? Whatever it was, marriage to Carol meant a new beginning, an end to his chaotic bachelor days and the start of the life he'd always dreamed of. Perhaps Robby had got fat or lost his hair and he wouldn't recognise him. In a way he hoped so. He felt none of the empathy twins were supposed to experience even over long periods of separation.

At the same time he looked forward to showing off his girl to his only living relative and, through his approval, validating the wisdom of his choice. He loved Carol for her cheerfulness and solid practicality. She had no interest in the darker side of things and as far as he could tell no experience of it either. The night terrors that had haunted him since childhood were unknown to her and she had none of his negativity that always saw the cup half empty. She could make or sew anything and had already fixed up the small house they'd bought in the suburbs and turned it into a cosy haven. Still, he worried his university-educated brother from England might find her a trifle 'homey'. And that was something he wouldn't endure.

The automatic doors opened to disgorge the first of the passengers. He examined each one as they came forward, unable to spot anyone who might be his brother. Then all at once he saw him. With his jeans and leather jacket and his face with that slightly peering expression, he was unmistakable. He felt a surge of emotion he was unprepared for as he stepped forward and embraced Robby in a bear hug.

In the car on the way home, the awkwardness quickly dissipated with all four of them speaking at once. Rich described the programme of outings he and Carol had prepared, designed partly, he admitted with an embarrassed laugh, in case they had nothing to say to each other. Carol had made a celebratory meal and afterwards they talked far into the night until Robby and Rosheen were overtaken by jetlag.

As they undressed for bed, Robby said to Rosheen, 'I wonder why I dreaded meeting Rich again? What was I so afraid of?'

'Perhaps because you'd once been so close.'

'It's true. At first I missed him so much it was like having an arm or a leg cut off. But after a while you just forget.'

'D'you wish you'd stayed here instead of leaving with your mother?'

'God, no! Life with my father was never a bed of roses.'

He reached for her and drew her into the bed.

'Besides I wouldn't have met you. My sane, beautiful girl!'

They kissed but were asleep before they could make love.

He woke in the night and as a result of the jetlag found it hard to get back to sleep, despite his exhaustion. He pressed himself into the warmth of Rosheen's body, listening to her quiet breathing as he held her close. The brightness that surrounded her thawed his chilly heart and, if she sensed the darkness within him, she did not speak of it. For that he was grateful and prayed that with time he would love her with the wholeheartedness that came so easily to her. Finally he drifted off, to wake once more with a throbbing erection and a savage desire.

The following morning he woke late and lay there enjoying the feeling of leisure. He observed Rosheen as she raised first one leg then the other to put on her jeans. There were bruises on the inside of her thigh and when she turned to pick up her teeshirt from the chair, he saw scratches on her breast. A vague feeling of unease moved within him. Sometimes, as in his dream of the woman on the plane who wasn't at all his type, he experienced feelings of such disturbing intensity they made him afraid. Awake, he harboured no sado-masochistic desires and it was inconceivable he could have harmed Rosheen in any way. Yet how had those marks got there? He remembered that they'd made love, passionately, but nothing rough or out of the ordinary. She'd never have tolerated that.

Sometimes, when he looked at his reflection in the bathroom mirror, he had the sickening impression that his features melted like wax and turned to fluid, until he disappeared like water down the plughole of the basin. The other night, when he lay in bed unable to sleep, the fear of dissolution had turned to panic that took a while to subside. He didn't mention any of this to Rosheen. It made him ashamed and he wouldn't have known how to describe it. Instead, he lay very still and imagined a train of camels as it made its way through the desert like a fleet of stately ships. The image never failed to calm him, and eventually the panic went away and he fell asleep. In the morning he felt normal again but, dreading a recurrence, he wondered if there might be something seriously wrong with him. Perhaps he could talk to Rich, who might have experienced something similar. He'd have to get him alone, which wouldn't be easy, and he had no idea how to introduce the subject. But it was worth a try.

He watched uneasily as Rosheen finished dressing then disappeared into the bathroom.

At breakfast Rosheen said she was feeling tired after the flight and wanted to take things easy. Robby tried to say something reassuring but she cut him short, declaring that all she needed was an early night. In an attempt to appear upbeat, he turned to Rich and asked what he'd got planned for his stag night.

'I don't do all night drinking and partying any more.'

'It doesn't have to be like that.'

'It does with me.'

'You've given up drinking?'

'The lot, man! Sex, drugs and rock and roll!'

'Since when?'

'Since the two of us got together.'

He put his arm around Carol, as she leaned across him to place a plate of pancakes on the table. His brother's uxoriousness was threatening to get on Robby's nerves.

'This woman's made me see the error of my ways. Isn't that right, honey?'

He smiled at her and she dropped a kiss on his head.

'I mean it's not as if a woman these days has to put up with a guy just because he puts food on the table.'

'Unlike our poor mother!'

Rich's smile faded.

'You sound just like him.'

'Like who?'

'Dad. He was good at sarcasm.'

'I guess life was pretty tough for him as well,' Robby said, doing his best to sound conciliatory. 'But sometimes I reckon he did things just to punish her for being who she was.'

He was thinking of his mother's remark that you can take the civilisation out of the savage but not the savage out of the so-called civilised person. He knew she was thinking of their father.

'That photo you sent of you and Dad on a hunting trip. You can't imagine how envious it made me in little old suburban England.'

'That was the last trip we took together.'

'He was already sick?'

Rich shrugged.

'Said he was tired of killing things, any rate... After he died I started going off on my own, sleeping rough, killing anything I came across. Like I'd inherited his addiction!'

'Perhaps that's what we should do for your stag weekend.'

'Go hunting?'

'Go to the mountains. Take a tent and whatever food we need. I remember some place with a river up north. We used to dive off the rocks. And there were loads of fish.'

Away from their parents on those trips, they'd always had a glorious time.

'It's never good to go back,' Rich said.

'Somewhere we've never been before then. Before you settle into your new life!'

'It'd be good to spend some time in the mountains, wouldn't it, Rich? Get to know one another again,' Carol encouraged.

Rich was silent. Eventually he said,

'Better turn in early then. It's a long drive.'

That night in their bedroom, Robby asked Rosheen if she minded being left on her own with Carol for a few days. Rosheen said she was looking forward to it. Carol had impressed her with her warmth and genuine concern for Rich's happiness, rather than seeking to change who he was. Still, Robby said, he feared the two of them might not have much in common. On the contrary, Rosheen retorted. She found Carol good company. They planned to do some shopping, which was an indulgence she rarely had time for, then visit a museum and take in a film. She made no reference to the marks on her body and he was too cowardly to mention them. He held her in his arms, hoping the gentleness of his caresses would erase whatever harm had been done. She made no attempt to push him away but he sensed a distance. Eventually he fell into a dreamless sleep and the following morning the two brothers set off before daylight, leaving the women still sleeping.

Rich scarcely spoke during the first part of the journey, which Robby put down to the earliness of the hour. He was driving and Robby stared out of the window, trying to locate any familiar landmarks as they travelled through the sleeping city, heading for the highway to Banff. The day was damp and overcast. Rich turned on the radio for the weather forecast, which promised an improvement during the course of the morning. Afterwards there was a programme of country music, hosted by the sort of homespun DJ Robby found intolerable. Eventually, after more than two hours of bouncing around uncomfortably in the battered jeep and his brother's silence, he was desperate for a break. He pointed out the signs for an approaching truck stop.

'Let's stop for a bite.'

'Carol made sandwiches and there's a thermos of coffee.'

Rich gestured behind him to the back seat.

'I need a pee.'

'Can't you hold it till we get to Banff?'

'No!'

Rich took the turn off at the last minute without cutting his speed so that the jeep barely made the curve and slewed to a halt in the parking area, narrowly missing another car.

'Jesus, man! Are you trying to turn this thing over?'

He'd had enough of his brother's surliness and badly needed the toilet. So much for his hope for some sort of confessional! He got out of the jeep and stomped angrily off in the direction of the diner.

Emerging from the gents, there was no sign of his brother. The place was virtually empty and he chose a table next to the window. He rubbed a hole in the steamy glass and saw Rich get out of the jeep and slouch his way across the tarmac. With his hunched shoulders and incipient paunch, he reminded Robby of a bear. He was beginning to think they should never have come.

The waitress appeared with the usual jug of tan coloured dishwater passing for coffee and he ordered a cheeseburger and fries. Rich entered and sat down opposite him but shook his head when the waitress asked what he wanted to eat.

'What's up?' Robby asked eventually.

'I don't see the point of wasting money in diners when there's perfectly good food in the car.'

'I told you. I needed a break. We've been on the road for hours.'

He ate in silence, too angry to relish his meal, whilst his brother sipped at the glass of water the waitress brought him.

Rich waited in the jeep, whilst Robby settled the check. When he returned, Robby suggested taking over the driving for a while. He shook his head and fired the engine into life. He'd known from the start that this trip was a mistake. Except for Carol urging him on, for his own peace of mind, to make a real effort to reconnect with his brother, he never would have embarked on it. For the first time in their relationship, Rich questioned her superior understanding of almost every situation. It was hardly surprising. She knew so little of their brief history together and failed, therefore, to see that the simplest thing by far was to let bygones be bygones and concentrate on the future.

Robby, on the other hand, revived by his breakfast, was in more generous mood. He stole a glance at his brother, frowning with the effort of concentration that reminded Robby of when he was a boy. He had taken off his hunting cap so that his thick brown hair lay flat on his scalp. He said nothing but then he'd never been much of a talker. No doubt he was finding their reunion as stressful as Robby, not to mention nerves about his forthcoming marriage. Meeting like this must stir up memories for him too, and not all of them good.

The sun had come out and in the streets and piazzas of Banff bright tubs of flowers announced a brief respite from the winter cold. Memories of visiting this and other tourist towns as a child filtered back to Robby, with familiar feelings of excitement about the approaching holiday. They would set out light-heartedly and then the fights would start. After a minor disagreement Rich, in revenge for Robby's greater skill at arguing, would throw up a wall of silence that blotted out his existence. It was an effective tactic and quickly provoked Robby into kicking and punching his brother, until their father stopped the car and gave them both a lathering. Even fear of his father couldn't curb Robby's rage whenever his brother resorted to this behaviour.

A door in his mind that had long been shut was creaking open and he began to recall other things. On what must have been their last trip around the time of their own eighth birthday, he had begun to realise how much his mother hated the forests and mountains of Canada. She was allergic to the legions of flies and mosquitoes that plagued them on every camping trip and refused to pluck or skin the dead creatures their father brought back from hunting. On that occasion she was so tense the slightest provocation would trigger a burst of anger out of all proportion. She didn't join in with their swimming or canoeing expeditions and spent most of the time reading in the tent. Years later when Robby asked her about those trips, she'd shuddered and retorted, 'They're behind me now, thank God. All those horrors!'

As they left the highway and headed up into the foothills, Rich seemed to relax.

'Less than an hour now and we turn up into the mountain.'

The going was tough, even for the jeep. Robby was pretty sure he hadn't been here before, though one part of these mountains looked very like another. The forest was a mixture of pine and deciduous trees, a feathery canopy through which the low sun winked. Higher up still there were only pines, until eventually the trees died out altogether, leaving bare rock that glowed apricot and indigo in the dying day. Below the road, a stream tumbled over boulders and the air smelled sharp and clear. The day had been warm but now was growing chilly. The sense of familiarity evoked by this landscape and the timeless endurance of rock and shale stirred in him a profound feeling of pleasure. Nothing he had ever experienced produced such an effect. It was, he now realised, what lay at the root of his love for geology.

'There's a place near here we can make camp. It won't take long to get a good fire going,' Rich said cheerfully.

Looking back on his brother's mood changes, Robby wondered if like their mother he suffered from depression. He'd often tried to imagine the life Rich had led up here in the woods, alone with their father who'd always been a hard, unpredictable man. His mother rarely spoke of Rich after they left, as if even the mention of his name was too painful. All he knew from their sporadic exchanges of postcards and phone calls, was that his brother had left home at seventeen to work on the fishing fleet out of Vancouver and hadn't returned until shortly before their father's death. He'd sent no word of that event until after the funeral. Their mother had learned of it from an old friend she'd kept up with in Calgary, and it occurred to Robby now that Rich might have been afraid she'd come over if she'd known in time. It was quite possible he didn't want to see her again and had never forgiven her for abandoning him.

Robby's own life by comparison had no doubt been stable and uneventful. After his A-levels he'd given up the idea of becoming a cartoonist and gone to Reading to study geology. The worst of his psychological problems was an over-attachment to his mother and subsequent difficulties in accommodating his replacement by a stepfather, or so the psychotherapist at the university told him. The way he saw it, any hostility he might have felt had been heavily outweighed by relief at having someone else to take his mother off his hands, and thus guarantee his freedom. It was only in the last year, after receiving his Ph.D had made urgent the choice between further academic work or a career in the field, that the panic attacks began.

They reached the clearing when it was almost dark. A crescent moon had appeared in a sky crowded with stars. They pitched the tent and Rich set about building a fire and directing Robby to bring the things from the jeep - frying pan, steaks, eggs, beans, and coffee. He'd thought of everything. Robby poured a measure of whisky into a mug and handed the flask to Rich.

'I told you. I don't drink any more. Besides food tastes better that way.'

The smell of frying meat made Robby realise how hungry he was.

Rich was in his element and Robby couldn't help admiring the practised way he carried out each action. He handed him a plate piled high, forked out another for himself, then squatted down beside the fire to eat.

'This life suits you.'

'Sure. But Carol's a city girl.'

'And that's where you're going to live?'

'There's no jobs up here. Besides it'll be far better for the kids. Time I settled to a regular life.'

'Perhaps you should take up painting again. People are always interested in nature and the wild and you've got the talent to capture those things. I always saw you as someone who needs to be close to them. Like Dad.'

Rich's expression darkened.

'Just 'cos I grew up like that, doesn't mean I'm like him.'

'I was thinking about them, Mum and Dad. How disastrous it was for two people with such different needs in life to have to share it. One or both were bound to end up being sacrificed.'

'It's not like that with us. Carol loves me and I can make her happy.'

'I don't doubt it. But if you don't like working at the factory, what are you going to do?'

'Did Carol say that?'

'She did, as a matter of fact.'

'There's plenty more jobs in Calgary.'

'If you've got a degree or a Ph.D. Otherwise it's something in a factory or an office, which you're no more suited to than Dad was.'

'I'm not him, for Chrissake!'

'I didn't mean you were. I'm concerned for you, that's all.'

'Well, don't be! Anyway, what's so great about your life? No kids and a woman you're afraid to commit to? All I want is to go to work in the morning and come home to my family at night. Is that such a bad ambition?'

'Of course not.'

Rich held out the saucepan with the last of the bacon and beans but Robby declined. He wanted to say more but words only seemed to increase the conflict. He reached for the dirty plates.

'I'll do these. You cooked.'

He walked over to the stream. He knew it was none of his business how his brother lived his life, and Rich had been right in what he'd said about his own existence. At least he and Carol shared a dream, whereas Robby had to admit he had no idea what Rosheen wanted, let alone himself.

His hands quickly grew numb in the liquid cold of the stream but he did his best to ignore it. He heard the rustling overhead as birds settled in for the night and somewhere far off a fox barked. Every sense felt alert and despite only a thin sliver of moon, he found he could see pretty well in the dark. Over in the clearing a log collapsed sending out a shower of sparks and the fire sputtered into flame. Rich had lit a lantern inside the tent, which glowed through the canvas. For the first time since arriving in Canada, Robby had a feeling of coming home.

When he returned to the fire, Rich had brewed coffee and handed him a mug into which he tipped the last of the whisky.

'D'you mind if I ask you something?'

Rich's expression was guarded but he nodded his assent.

'Did Dad ever have another woman after Mum left?'

'Not that I know of. '

'Was he hard on you?'

Rich shrugged.

'He belted me once in a while. Mostly when he was drunk.'

'But he looked after things? The house, meals and that?'

'You kidding? Housekeeping was never his forte! What he cared for was hunting, living like a backwoodsman. One summer we took off for the mountains and by the time we got back to town, school was halfway done. The authorities served him a court order and he had to promise it wouldn't happen again else I'd be taken in by the social.'

'Did he stick to it?'

Rich laughed.

'It gave him the excuse he needed to go back up north. Somewhere where school, if there was one, didn't bother about things like attendance.'

'Did you mind that? Missing out on school?'

'Hell, no! What boy likes school? I was never much for grades and things... Unlike you.'

'Sometimes I wonder if the reason I studied geology was to come back here. Often I dreamed of a prospecting job, somewhere up north.'

'I guess it's in the blood.'

'Not on the maternal side!'

The fire was dying down. Robby shivered, feeling the bite of the cold mountain air.

'I'm whacked! Mind if I turn in?'

He fell asleep in the warmth of his sleeping bag but after a few hours, the cold woke him again. He reached for the flask he'd brought into the tent before remembering it was empty, then rummaged in his backpack for an extra sweater. It was still dark but he could hear his brother's irregular breathing. He must have been dreaming because suddenly he gave a cry, so anguished that Robby reached over to shake him awake. As his hand touched his shoulder, Rich jerked round and grabbed it with his teeth. Robby wrenched his hand away and stumbled out of the tent.

His hand was throbbing and, peering closer, he could see marks where the teeth had drawn blood. He went to the stream and let the icy water numb the pain, too shocked to know what to feel. The thought of getting back into the tent was unbearable so he grabbed his sleeping bag and spent the rest of the night in the jeep.

The following morning was bright and clear, with the promise of a warm day. Robby woke from an uncomfortable sleep to find Rich demanding to know why he'd abandoned the tent. It was clear he had no memory of what he'd done and it wasn't until later, when he passed Robby a mug of coffee, he asked him about his bandaged hand. Robby replied that he'd caught it on some poison ivy down by the stream, which might also explain his seeming out of sorts. Half of him wanted to pack up at once and return to Calgary. But something more insistent drove him on. They ate breakfast in silence, packed up the gear they weren't taking with them into the jeep, and set off on foot.

The air was fragrant with the scent of pines and the path, edged with low bushes weighed down with blueberries, was soft underfoot. The sun filtered in onto the forest floor in long shafts, releasing the dank scent of the earth and casting yellow pools where small blue and white flowers floated in drifts. It seemed to Robby an enchanted Eden.

They took off their jackets and stuffed them in their backpacks. Walking in single file, they talked little. Rich loped along with effortless stride as if he could keep going all day. For Robby the going was harder, what with the weight on his back and the reduced oxygen because of the altitude. Eventually, feeling hungry, they stopped to eat and afterwards stretched out on the warm ground. Rich curled up on his side and fell asleep at once with his head on his arm. He so resembled the boy Robby remembered, that for a moment he was overwhelmed by grief for lost time. What would have happened if they'd remained together? Would that have prevented the horrors he felt sure his brother had had to endure? Deep down he'd always believed himself, younger than his brother by ten minutes, to be the favoured one, the one who'd escaped.

As Rich went on sleeping, Robby grew restless. He got up, intending to walk a little further down the track before returning. A path led off to the left that was quickly lost to sight among the trees. On an impulse he followed it and emerged into a sunlit clearing. On the far side was a cottage, little more than a cabin really, surrounded by an unruly garden and a white picket fence. From where he stood he could smell the flowers and hear the drone of bees. He went closer and pushed open the gate. A path went between tall hollyhocks half choked with bindweed and heavily scented nicotiana to a stout oak door. The place looked empty but he knocked all the same.

There was no sound from within so he knocked again, then walked round to a window and peered in. A shabby but homely room occupied most of the ground floor, into which the front door opened directly. It had a wooden floor, a dilapidated blue sofa, an armchair and some upright chairs around a once handsome, maplewood table. On the table he could see a battered biscuit tin decorated with toy soldiers in red uniforms and a tea-stained mug. A threadbare native Indian rug lay in front of the fireplace and there were ashes in the hearth. He turned from the window and as he did so, his foot kicked over a flowerpot of red and yellow nasturtiums. Beneath it was a key. Robby picked it up, went to the front door and tried it in the lock. The door opened.

Fragments of memory jostled for recognition before slipping back below the surface of his consciousness. He felt giddy and seized hold of the edge of the table for support. His gaze fell on the biscuit tin with its army of tiny soldiers and another jolt of déjà vu hit him like an electric shock. In their chipped red uniforms, jumping to attention and brandishing miniature muskets, they were uncannily familiar. He reached for the tin, dislodging the lid and releasing a stale, biscuity odour.

Inside was nothing but crumbs. He scooped them up greedily then replaced the tin on the table and turned to the fireplace.

On the mantelpiece above the fire there was a small flowered jug with the name 'Sybil' in flowing gold letters. Sybil was his mother's name. He repeated the soft, sibilant sound under his breath and shuddered as he did so. The fog that was filling his brain seemed also to be invading his body, turning his knees weak. He groped his way to the armchair and collapsed, closing his eyes.

When Rich woke, for a moment he forgot that he wasn't alone as usual. Then he remembered. His brother must have got bored and walked on. He was pretty sure he knew where to find him. After all, wasn't that the reason he'd brought him here?

Robby woke to find the sun low in the sky. He heard footsteps and the door opened to reveal a man silhouetted against the brightness, bearing an armful of kindling. He blinked his eyes and recognised his brother.

'You found it then.'

Rich dumped their two rucksacks on the floor and went over to the fireplace to deposit his wood. He began raking the ashes.

'It'll be more comfortable here than sleeping on the cold ground.'

Robby, dazed from sleep, watched him coax the wood into flames.

'You know this place?'

'I use it from time to time.'

Robby glanced over at the posturing soldiers on the biscuit tin.

'Did we come here as children?'

Rich did not reply.

'Speak to me, man!'

His brother's silence ignited his old frustration.

'That mug on the mantlepiece, it's got Mum's name on it.'

'Yes.'

'Is that all you can say?'

The sun was almost gone. The last dregs stained the floor boards the colour of blood orange. From somewhere far off an animal cried out, more of a howl than a cry. Rich lifted his head and Robby felt a prickle of fear.

'Something happened here, didn't it?'

His voice sounded strange in his ears as if it belonged to someone else.

Rich remained mute.

'Answer me, goddammit!'

It was all he could do to stop himself from jumping up and grabbing him by the throat. Rich turned to him. He seemed to be having difficulty with his words.

'The last time we were here ... it was with Dad. She'd refused to come, like she always did.'

'How old were we?'

'Five, maybe six.'

'And when we got back they had a terrible row. I remember. I woke in the night and came downstairs.'

Memories stirred to life in the depths of his consciousness.

'They were always rowing.'

'No. This was different. I'd had this awful dream. It felt like the world was collapsing round me and I was tumbling down an endless vortex. I needed her to comfort me so I went downstairs and I saw them. She was throwing herself around the room and shouting like a crazy woman.'

'And him?'

'He tried to quieten her but she kept on screaming. "Four days they were gone!" like it was all his fault.... What happened?'

'Don't you remember anything?'

Robby shook his head. Rich was silent for a moment.

'We were here in this cottage. You were crying how you wanted to go home. Dad told you to shut up but you wouldn't. Eventually he took off his belt to give you a thrashing but you wriggled free and hid under the table.'

Recollection lurched in Robby like a tide of seasickness - fear of his father overwhelmed by a deeper terror, the panic that his mother would go away as she'd always threatened and wouldn't be there when he got home. From under the table he watched, paralysed, as his father's boots strode back and forth over the worn carpet. His father shouted, 'Come out, you little bastard, or I'll not answer for myself!' He did not move but clutched the biscuit tin with the soldiers to his chest, fighting for breath. His father lost patience. He dragged him out and shook him like a rat, calling him a pathetic milksop he was ashamed to call son. Robby gasped back that he hated his father and wished he were dead and waited for the blow to fall. Suddenly his brother was there. Rich butted his father's knees from behind so that he let go of Robby and crumpled to the ground. Rich grabbed Robby's hand and together they flew out of the door and down the path to the forest.

Through the gate and into the woods they ran in a headlong rush, crashing through the undergrowth and stumbling over tree roots in the blinding dark. The stench of panic filled Robby's nostrils and his heart was ready to burst from his chest, but they ran and ran until their legs bore them up no longer and their strength gave out. They sank down under a tree and huddled together for warmth.

He could smell the grave-like scent of wet leaves as he fought against the dead weight that threatened to crush the last of his breath out of him. They were lost in a limitless darkness, yet all around them things were on the move. He felt the swift caress of a bird's wing as it swooped towards its prey, and heard the sounds of night creatures rustling in the undergrowth as they went about their nocturnal business. Closer at hand, the rhythmic gnawing of insect mandibles and dry slither of a snake over dead leaves sent prickles along his skin. They had reached the very heart of the forest, where no one would ever find them because no human being dared penetrate this far. They might die of hunger and thirst but they were safe.

Panic gave way to a Lethe-like lethargy and he began to breathe more freely. His hyper-sensitised hearing picked up a soft padding footfall. But he made no move to flee, nor to resist the rough maternal embrace that engulfed him, suffocating in its rankness. Instead he pressed himself into the coarse pelt where the inhuman heart beat faster than his own, as his greedy mouth nuzzled across the mottled belly, seeking out a soft protuberance until it found it and sucked down hard. Milk flooded his throat, filling his body with blissful warmth. The nagging pain of separation, and with it all fear, melted in the heat of a love fiercer and more pure than any he had ever known, and he was at peace.

Robby sat very still in his chair. The least move might dislodge his memory and tip him back into the desert of forgetfulness. Like lost treasure unearthed, he clutched it to him, feeling his fears grow insubstantial as shameful yearnings that could never be fulfilled were pardoned.

The howling came again, only this time closer. His heart beat faster but the constriction in his chest had gone and he breathed freely. Everything in his life had been leading up to this moment. His brother got up and flung wide the door, so that a beam of light from the room flooded out onto the path. Robby stood beside him, peering into the night. As he grew accustomed to the dark, he could make out a ghostly shape between the trees, its eyes yellow as topaz, and joy flooded through him.

*　*　*

Rich waved one last time as Robby and Rosheen made their way through the security gates at the airport. His secret, for so long borne alone, was now shared, though it was unlikely he and his brother would ever speak of it again nor had he any wish to do so. He would never know if the unearthing of that carefully buried memory would provide ease to Robby, as it had to himself. His brother was no longer his affair. It was time to move on, to concentrate on his life with Carol and, with luck, on the family they would raise together.

He closed his eyes briefly and when he reopened them, no trace of his brother or Rosheen remained. He threaded his arm through Carol's and together they made their way back towards the exit.

Robby and Rosheen settled into their seats, preparing for the long night ahead. Travelling due north promised a vision of dawn as it rose over the Arctic and turned its pristine surface pink and gold. Once more they were seated in the middle row with little room to spare. But despite the discomfort, the hours of darkness ahead gave him the opportunity he sought. It was time to tell Rosheen, if he could find the words, what was in his heart.

He took her hand.

'Carol's good for Rich, don't you think? I reckon they'll be happy,' she said.

'I hope so. At first I thought it's disastrous. He'll never be able to settle down.'

She laughed.

'It's more the other way round. He's longing for it. If anyone feels pressured, it's her.'

'Really?'

It wasn't the first time he'd realised how little he understood about other people compared to Rosheen. He wasn't really interested, though that didn't make him proud.

'Stupid the way we take things for granted about people.'

'Especially about women!'

'Yes.'

He hesitated for a moment.

'What is it you want, Rosheen?'

'In a man?'

'That too.'

She considered for a moment.

'Someone who's not afraid to tell the truth, no matter what secrets he's got. And the trust that comes from honesty.'

'And if those secrets are shameful?'

'It's a risk I'd take.'

His mind went back to the high dives of his childhood, hovering up there on the cliff as his brother leapt, fearless.

'It's a long story,' he said eventually.

She squeezed his hand,
'We've got all night.'

Phoenix

'Rosheen! You're back! It's Lola. How was the trip?'
    'Canada's amazing! I'll tell you all. When can we meet?'

    'Thing is, I'm about to catch a train to Scotland. I was wondering, could you look after Fergus for a few weeks?'

    'OK. But what about the bank?'

'I quit.'

'You haven't done something stupid?'

'Quite likely! I was probably going to get the push anyway with this financial crisis.'

'Still, it's a job.'

'I'd more or less made up my mind and then this guy turned up.'

'What d'you mean? What guy?'

'He turned up at the office the other day. He claims we know each other and now he's saying my grandfather promised him his diary before he died. He's demanding I hand it over.'

'Whoa! You're not making sense.... Is he with you now? '

'He was. I told him to piss off. It's weird. He seems to know all about my family.'

'And you never met him before? D'you even know what diary he's talking about?'

'No! That's the funny part. He says Grandpa wrote it during the Second World War in India. He could be making it up, for all I know.'

'I think you should tell the police, Lola.'

'Tell them what? He's not dangerous! Anyway, if this diary exists, it'll be in Scotland. Grandpa left me the house in his will. I've been meaning to sort the place out and now's the time to do it.'

'But should you go on your own? I mean, what if this guy follows you?'

'I always go on my own.'

'Well, call me as soon as you get there.'

'I'll try. But the mobile connection's unreliable and I didn't pay the bill so the landline's probably cut off.'

'So find a phone box or an internet café.'

'In Marne? You must be joking!... They just announced the train. I better run.'

'If you don't call, I'll come up myself! And don't worry about the cat.'

*   *   *

From the diary of Major Jake Mullen, 1944-45.

October 12th, 1944.
Fort Wana, Waziristan. India.

Riding for the first time into these wild hills with a company of cavalry, I thought of the ironies of war. Whatever the dangers and hardships, for me as for many others, it has proved a liberation. Were it not for the army, I would still be making the daily trek across London Bridge to my place of bondage in the city and counting the days to my retirement. Now in one of the most remote and unruly corners of the British Empire and at twenty six the youngest Major in the battalion, I daily count my blessings!

Social life at the fort is limited to the handful of British and Indian officers who inhabit it and the surrounding settlements, overseen by the Regional Commander. Yesterday I was invited for a khanna, an evening of feasting, by Abdul Qadir, the civil link between the tribes in this region and the army's Political Department.

The Tahail where he lives with his staff, his kassadars and bedraggas, is a small, fortified settlement just outside the perimeter wire of Wana. Also invited were the Assistant Political Agent, Captain Mohamed, Yusuf Khan, a couple of the Brigade officers and myself. A copious spread of roasted meats and fruit of all kinds accompanied by green tea (no alcohol since they are Mohammedans), had been laid out for us, so much it would have taken a whole company to do justice to it. One reclines on rugs and cushions beside a great log fire as the nights up here can be bitterly cold.

Conversation circled around questions of a philosophical or religious nature. Yusuf Khan spoke of his meeting the previous day with a Pir from Gul Kach and their discussion of happiness, or rather its negation since according to the Pir happiness doesn't exist. Captain Mohamed begged to disagree. Although not all his prayers are answered, he said, great happiness is to be found by doing good and considering others. Yusuf declaimed against the ignorant tribesman and his superstitious practice of worshipping at shrines. Approaching the Divine Power via an intermediary apparently goes entirely against the teachings of the Koran. I retorted rather facetiously that in that case the entire Christian Church would be out of a job and caught the look of amusement on Abdul's face. He declared, to general shock and consternation, that since prayer in these days is not answered there seems little use in praying at all. I find him increasingly interesting.

Today I had arranged to go on a reconnaissance mission and invited Abdul, who is also my political scout, to accompany me, together with a small attachment of soldiers. When we reached Gul Kach where the grazing route follows the Gumal River, we met with an incredible sight. A great multitude of men, women and children with their horses, goats and camels were flowing down from the hills on the far side of the river into the valley. Their bright robes illuminated the arid landscape with an explosion of colour. The sight of so many, travelling with such oneness of purpose yet no discernable order, was strangely moving. 'Ah,' said Abdul, noticing my reaction, 'you have seen the Children of Israel!' I asked him who they were and he replied that they were the Dotannis, a nomadic people making their yearly pilgrimage to their winter pasturage. It is a vision I shall not easily forget.

November 2nd, 1944.
Fort Wana.

Life here is wholly removed from anything I have known before, even in India. But there are times when I feel isolated and would welcome the company of my own kind to chew things over with, especially as I'm beginning to realise the problems of the region may be even more intractable than I'd thought. As it is, I must maintain a certain distance from the men in order to keep their respect, especially since many of them are older and far more experienced than me. And with the Commanding Officer, who is a career officer, I must know my place.

The nearest I have to a friend is Abdul Qadir. He is a cultivated man, despite having lived in these remote regions all his life. He is also unusually tall and light-skinned for an Indian, though that is not so unusual amongst the tribes along the Afghan border who have Persian blood. Yesterday we went hunting for jackal in the early morning. I can't describe the feeling of liberation I experienced after the imprisonment of the fort as we galloped over the undulating ground once the hounds had caught the scent, flying over low walls and irrigation ditches.

On the way back we fell to talking. Commenting on my previous low spirits, Abdul suggested I join him for a musical evening. Not your usual boogeywoogeywallah, he explained, but traditional music played by the finest musicians with such skill and passion that he guaranteed my enjoyment. I agreed, though more out of gratitude for the diversion than any expectation of pleasure.

We fell to talking of music in general and I asked him whether his tastes extended to western styles. To my surprise, he described a trip to England for a Scout Jamboree. In London he discovered a small shop in the Edgware Road, run by a Bengali. The first record he bought there was 'Serenade Espagnol', which appealed to him on account of its exotic name. From there he went on to rumbas and tangos, exhausting all his meagre funds. Back in India, he came across a radiogram in the officers' mess and began to entertain the company with his collection, which by then included

Strauss and Liszt. I asked what had happened to all these records and if he still had them. 'Most of them are at home with my wife,' he replied, 'But I carry a box of favourites, together with a portable gramophone wherever I go.' The first I'd heard of a wife! I asked if I might hear them sometime, to which he agreed. The more I get to know this man, the more he surprises me.

Re-entering the perimeter fence we passed the hockey pitch and polo ground and I formed the idea of gathering together a team of our men for a match. But who would you play, Abdul inquired. I replied that the local tribes already come from all over on Saturdays and are only too keen to take on any challenger. For the duration of the match they suspend their hostilities with rival clans and fight it out fair and square on the pitch. But no sooner the sun begins to sink and play stops, than they ride like hell to get clear of the fort and resume shooting one another. Abdul laughed and remarked how their inexhaustible appetite for skirmishing makes our mission to pacify them rather pointless. I replied that if that's so it's a sentiment best kept from the C.O.

In fact it is becoming clearer to me each day what a Promethean task we have set ourselves here. The three main tribes are the Khel clans, the most powerful of which is the Ganghi Khel and the smallest and least powerful, the Toji Khel. Today I learned that the Toji Khel have been making up for their lack of strength by copying our Lee Enfield rifles, with considerable skill it is said, and selling them to anyone who'll buy. Thus they have succeeded in arming half the tribesmen in the hills. Rounding up such illegal arms would involve excavating the floor of every cave and wretched hovel and even if one had the whole Allied Army to carry it out, there is a further problem. If one tribe were successfully disarmed, its rival would simply seize the opportunity to massacre it. Such are the blood feuds and ancient quarrels amongst the clans, the origins of which no one either remembers or cares about.

Yet there is much to love about this place, especially the trust between the men rarely met with in less challenging circumstances. It is my hopes of making a difference or at least some small contribution to the resolution of this great conflict, which take the biggest knock.

December 1st, 1944.
Fort Wana, India.

I have now attended my third of Abdul's musical evenings and am getting quite a taste for them. There are usually three or four other guests and a group of four musicians playing tablas, veena and scitar. Songs are sung in Pushto, Persian and Urdo and we listeners recline comfortably on cushions.

Though at first I found it hard to concentrate, the music being so alien to my ear, gradually as I have become more accustomed to it I am able to distinguish different motifs and to follow some of the incredibly complex changes of rhythm. This last evening I reached a state of virtual trance, losing all sense of my surroundings and being filled with an intense calm, the like of which I have never experienced. At the end of the evening I thanked Abdul whole-heartedly and he appeared delighted by my enthusiasm. It is on occasions such as this, when I get some insight into the real culture of these people, that it all seems worthwhile.

Sometimes I think I have never felt so alive as I do now, despite all the hardships and the isolation. Each day I awake with a sense of expectancy, especially if I am to spend part of it in the company of Abdul Qadir. At times I wonder if I am becoming too dependant on his friendship and whether the pleasure I find in being with him is reciprocated. I hate to think it is just some stupid schoolboy crush. But whatever it is, these feelings and the accompanying zest for life are wholly new. I have known nothing similar, even in the early days of courting Mary, though it pains me to say so. Perhaps I am not cut out for marriage. Sometimes, in the dark hours of the night, I fear I am incapable of the manly love required of a husband.

December 10th, 1944.
Fort Wana, Waziristan.

This morning the fragile peace we have been enjoying was shattered. One of the workers on the irrigation project at the place known as Shinwarsuk, or Green Spur because of its unusual holly and evergreen trees, was shot and killed. There have been skirmishes up there before between rival clans and the Afghan workers but nothing serious since it is widely known that the project is funded by the government, with armed guards in constant attendance. I gathered some men together and rode up there at once, pausing only to pick up Abdul as my interpreter.

It turns out that the dead man is not one of the Afghans who are in charge of designing the system of wells but a member of the Ganghi Khel, who dig the irrigation ditches and provide most of the labour. The tribesmen were up in arms and it took a lot of careful diplomacy before they would agree to talk to me. Eventually I learned that the Toji Khel have been threatening the workers for some time, out of jealousy for their wages. It is they whom the Ganghi Khel are accusing of the murder.

Whilst I was talking with the tribesmen, Abdul who speaks fluent Persian as well as Pushto, was questioning the Afghan workers and came up with quite a different story. He asked them if they had seen the killer and they replied that they had and indeed they recognised him. He was the famous bandit, Mazrak. Abdul asked why a bandit would want to shoot a worker under the protection of the army and was told that he wished to create a diversion from his own activities by exploiting the rivalry between the Khel tribes. In short, he is aiming to start a clan war.

Later as I sat in my turret room, watching the rugs on the stone flags lifting in the fierce gusts that blew in under the door and listening to the wind howl in the chimney, I tried to think about how to deal with this mess. Soon it will be Christmas and the men are expecting some relaxation of duty over the festive season, when what is called for is a full red alert. I have to admit I am rather out of my depth and the whole thing is too volatile to make mistakes. Eventually I fell asleep at my desk and was woken a couple of hours later by the cold.

I have spent today questioning workers from the irrigation site and some of the soldiers of the guard. The Afghans' story appears the most plausible, not least since they are less involved in local feuding. But if the bandit Mazrak is responsible for the killing, the Ganghi Khel are still insisting that the Toji Khel put him up to it and want revenge.

December 13th, 1944.
Fort Wana, Waziristan.

I had just returned to my quarters when a soldier burst in, announcing they had brought in a prisoner. I went down to the guard room where to my amazement I found a bedraggled young woman dressed in a belted skirt, her hair hidden under a cap and a ripped, stained blanket around her shoulders. Despite her obvious exhaustion, she fixed me with a fierce, defiant gaze but refused to speak a word. I told the men to give her some food and let her stew till morning. When she had been removed to a cell, I asked what was the reason for her capture and was told that she was the outlaw Mazrak's daughter. One of the tribesmen had caught her hiding in a cave in the hills. Of the father there is as yet no sign.

December 14th, 1944.
Fort Wana.

This morning I went down to the guard room to interview the prisoner, taking with me an interpreter in the hope that she might be in a mood to answer my questions. When the interpreter started to translate my words, she spoke up and declared in passable English that she had no need of him and wished this interview to be between the two of us. I dismissed the interpreter but could get very little out of her, other than to protest her innocence and declare that her father would not take kindly to her imprisonment. I told her that the army was more likely to respond to cooperation than threats then decided that little more was to be gained by prolonging the interview so ordered her back to her cell. Before she went she asked a favour, which I agreed to if it was within the bounds of law. She replied that she wanted something to pass the time and requested the stories of Saki. I told her that if the fort library had a copy, it would be in English and she said that was fine. Whether or not this is just bravado, I will make a point of tracking a copy down.

Shortly after I had returned to my quarters, the sergeant who had brought in the prisoner came to see me. He was in a state of some excitement and needed no encouragement to burst out with his idea. He's been asking around about the outlaw and his daughter, he said, and learned that she often rides with him. Such a thing is highly unusual for a woman in these parts, which is why it has attracted such attention. In fact she is considered by many to be his partner in crime. The sergeant's plan is to charge her with being an accessory to the killing and since the penalty for murder is death, for the sake of his honour and the love he is known to bear her, Mazrak is bound to surrender himself to spare his daughter. I told him I would think it over but agreed it is a good plan and the sergeant went away pleased with himself.

But no sooner had I settled down to write a report on the matter for the C.O. than I received another interruption, this time from Abdul Qadir. I got up to greet him but he brushed me aside. He'd heard I had the outlaw Mazrak's daughter in the cells and wanted to know if it was true. His manner was brusque to the point of rudeness, something I have never encountered in him before. I replied rather coldly that it was but I didn't see what business it was of his. He demanded to know what the charge was. My temper flared up at his insistence and before I could stop myself, I told him that he was out of line and ordered him from the fort. He hesitated for a moment then, without a word, turned on his heel and left. As I heard his boots descending the stone steps and his voice calling for the guard in the courtyard below, I found myself shaking with anger.

Later that evening my dinner was interrupted by a soldier, who handed me a note. It was from Abdul, apologising for his earlier rudeness and asking when he could see me to explain his behaviour. I am still too angry to reply. Instead I went to the library to look for the copy of Saki for Mazrak's daughter and eventually managed to track one down. It is too late to give it to her tonight but I will deliver it in the morning.

December 16th, 1944.
Fort Wana.

Her name is Raza Mazrak and she received the book with unexpected graciousness. She is not a beautiful woman, being too small and dark skinned for our European taste. But she has a vivacity about her which is striking, and sometimes when she talks her face lights up with a mischievous intelligence. She is surprisingly well educated, though how she came by it I can't imagine. She asked me on what grounds I was keeping her locked up and I explained that since she is known to ride with her father, she will be charged as his accomplice unless he gives himself up. She thought about this then thanked me for my frankness. She is in her way quite an unusual young woman.

I was completing my report to the C.O., when my orderly informed me that Abdul was in the courtyard asking to see me. Feeling more rational by this time, I told him to let him up. Without preliminaries, Abdul apologised for his previous rudeness and asked if I had interviewed Raza Mazrak yet and what I intended to do with her. I replied that I had informed her that I was holding her as an accessory to her father's killing of an irrigation worker. She had been seen riding with him on the morning of the shooting and was later found hiding in a cave not far from the irrigation works. Making a visible effort to control himself, Abdul protested that riding with her father was in itself no crime and that unless a weapon had been found on her, what evidence was there to convict her of murder. I said that was a matter for the trial.

'What if her father doesn't show up?' he demanded. 'It's obvious that avoiding a clan war is far more important to you than an innocent human being's life!'

I replied quite calmly that the choice was Mazrak's. According to the law, if he is found guilty either he takes his punishment or his accomplice must answer for his crime. At this Abdul exploded with rage.

'Is this your fabled British justice?' he shouted. 'What parody of law offers up the life of an innocent young woman as scapegoat?'

'Good God, man!' I retorted. 'To hear you, anyone would think you were in love with this woman!'

He glared at me and said through his teeth, 'She is my life and soul!'

I almost laughed out loud. His words were like something out of a cheap novel. I said, somewhat priggishly, that I understood he was already a married man, to which he replied that as a Mohammedan he was allowed more than one wife. On his way out, he turned back and said,

'If it's a scapegoat you want, then take me!'

'The rules of the British justice which you so despise don't allow innocent volunteers to take the place of the guilty,' I returned calmly.

He turned on his heel and left.

December 22nd, 1944.
Fort Wana.

It is nearly Christmas and a big bash is to be held at the fort on Christmas Eve. The men are full of preparations. Raza Mazrak is still in the cells and there has been no word from her father, though we have spread the news of her capture far and wide. So much for the man of honour!

I have not seen or heard from Abdul Qadir since his visit here and now that my anger has settled, I regret the high-handed way I treated him. Even though his interference was out of order.

I have been largely confined to quarters because of a cold and the bitter weather, which has made it virtually impossible to leave the fort even for a gallop across the wadi. What with the lack of exercise and only myself for company, the hours drag and I find it hard to settle to anything despite all the reports and letters home that need writing. It's over a month since I wrote to Mary and the realisation that she will receive nothing from me for Christmas is a source of guilt. Now that she has the child to occupy her, she has more to do than worry about me but that doesn't excuse my negligence. Being so far away means that she can have little idea or interest in the goings-on here but the truth is that I have given up trying to explain things to her. She and I never talked much about our intimate feelings and the few occasions we tried seemed to cause more bewilderment than closeness. Sometimes, with the war coming to an end, I wonder about the future and returning to England. The war has changed everything, not least England itself, which no longer seems like home. Perhaps I should remain in India, get a teaching post or start up a business. Then I remind myself that I am no longer a free man and such thoughts are out of the question.

Before I retired for the night I went to check on Mazrak's daughter, having heard she was refusing food. I couldn't help thinking of Abdul's declaration and looked at her with new eyes. She is undoubtedly a formidable young woman, though lacking the physical beauty that usually inspires such devotion. She has nothing of the charm or submissiveness we British associate with femininity, nor the sensuality of many Indian women. She lacks all airs and graces and seems to have been raised more like a son by her father, though she is not mannish.

December 23rd, 1944.
Fort Wana.

I increasingly miss the almost daily conversations with Abdul, though I no longer know what I would say to him. He seems incapable of accepting even the possibility of Raza Mazrak being complicit in her father's deeds and is blind to the responsibility I bear to the army and the necessity of avoiding a clan war. All this makes it clear how little he values our friendship. But whatever hurt I feel, I must not allow it to influence my judgement or affect the rationality of my decisions.

* * *

Translation in Jake's handwriting of a letter marked: 'Original written in Persian and hand-delivered to Fort Wana.
Dated December 24ᵗʰ, 1944 and addressed to 'The Prisoner'.
(Found amongst Jake Mullen's papers.)

My dearest wife, keeper of my soul,

I write to you in our own language to deter the prying eyes of those who would harm you. To think of you in that dingy cell is like imagining the caged falcon whose element is the wild sky. My innocent bird, you know that I will lay down my life to keep you free from harm.

I have bided my time, waiting to hear if your father has sent word. But there is no message and I am unable to discover his whereabouts. Therefore it is time to take the future into our own hands. We must act without fear.

Major Mullen, whom I considered to be my friend, has proved true to his tribe and thinks only of his duties as our master. Nevertheless, he can be brought to serve our need. I have observed how he looks at me and know the special place I occupy in his heart, feelings that he will never speak of since in his culture they are a cause for great shame. In the name of this friendship, I will persuade him to act upon his own authority and secure your release.

My fears, my bird, are not for your lack of courage but for my own. My love for you shall not make me cautious nor must the selfishness of my desire overwhelm my judgement concerning your wellbeing.

Send me word that you are in good heart.
Your ever faithful husband and lover, Abdul.

*   *   *

From Jake Mullen's Diary

December.2
6th, 1944. Fort Wana. Waziristan.

The Christmas party was a great success. The men ate and drank to excess and dinner was followed by games organised by one of the sergeants. They started with charades and ended up with riotous bouts of blind man's buff and musical chairs. During the games Abdul sought me out and asked if he could have a word in private so we went to my office.

He began by saying he regretted his outspoken behaviour and recognised the difficulty of my position. Given the urgency of the situation, he went on, he had come up with a plan. He will go to the Ganghi Khel and offer himself as hostage for the outlaw, Mazrak, in place of Raza. He is sure that as Mazrak's intended son-in-law and a soldier under the British army, he will make a more prized hostage. I replied that though this might satisfy the clans, it would be unlikely to force the real culprit to show up if he'd failed to do so for his daughter. Abdul retorted that Mazrak's honour and his position as head of his clan would be intolerably compromised if he allowed his daughter's husband to take his place. In the end, unable to come up with any reasonable objection, I agreed, providing both the Khel clans accept the arrangement and subject to the approval of the C.O. He seemed much relieved and congratulated me on my 'British pragmatism'. I could think of no suitably light remark in response and ignored the profound unease I felt.

'When this is all over, we'll celebrate with a real boogeywoogeywallah!' Abdul said cheerfully as he left.

Is it too late to forbid him to go?

December 29th, 1944.
Fort Wana

The locals being no respecters of Christmas, skirmishing continues. This time one of the strategic routes we are constructing with tribal labour was attacked by paid hostiles of the Faqir of Ipi, a known troublemaker. No sooner had I assigned armed guards to the site and returned to the fort than there was news of the bandit Mazrak being seen near the northern edge of the cultivation, but it turned out to be a false alarm. All this means that I have not yet written to the C.O. about Abdul's plan to offer himself as hostage to the Ganghi Khel and now I learn that he, the C.O., has gone down to Rawalpindi for the New Year. On reflection, this may be no bad thing, since it will delay any action on Abdul's part.

January 1st, 1945.
Fort Wana.

The blackest day of my life! I can scarcely bring myself to write down what has happened. Two hours ago a scout arrived at the fort with the news that the Ganghi Khel have put their hostage, Abdul Qadir, to death in retribution for the killing of one of their tribesmen.

There is only myself to blame. I deliberately delayed informing the C.O. in the face of what I knew to be true, that Abdul would care nothing for the army's permission when it came to offering himself up on behalf of the woman he loves. Perhaps I am unable to accept the existence of such a love, in comparison to which his life meant little to him. Whatever the truth of it, I am responsible for my friend's death and I must live with this knowledge for the rest of my days.

* * *

(Notebook found with Jake Mullen's papers and written by his daughter, Beryl Mullen, between March and May 1956)

On the cover: 'This diary belongs to Beryl Mullen. Strictly Private.

March 1956, Cheam, England, Europe, the World, the Universe, near Mars.'

All morning I've been revising in my freezing bedroom. Winter's returned and it's so cold I can see my breath and my fingers won't hold the pen. I put on the fingerless gloves Auntie Gwen knitted me for Christmas but they don't help. I'll have to go down to the kitchen, even though it's Mrs Cuttles' day and she has the wireless on the whole time, FULL BLAST! I hate Victor Sylvester!

When I complain to Mummy about the cold in my bedroom, she says I have to grin and bear it or come downstairs, though the sitting room's not much warmer. The electric fire has only one bar working and we're not allowed to light a fire during the week because of coal rationing. She says Daddy refuses to pay for proper heating so even the cold turns out to be his fault! Sometimes I hate her for her complaining. Perhaps if she wasn't so angry with him all the time, he'd visit us more often and see for himself how horrible this house is.

I've been invited to go on a cycling tour of Holland with Ginny and her parents and little brother this Easter and Mummy has agreed to let me go if Daddy pays for my share. It's the first time I've been anywhere by myself but Ginny's father is a QC so she approves of him. Little does she know how he chases me round the garden whenever he gets the chance, making his big bear noises and trying to pull my hair. If the whole family wasn't going I wouldn't, even if it does mean a chance to see the world. But I mustn't complain. I know Mummy does her best to see that I want for nothing. The trouble is, she doesn't really know what I want.

April 1st, 1956.
Cheam, England.

The Holland trip is looking increasingly uncertain. Daddy hasn't yet sent the money and though the Blakemores have offered to let us pay them back on our return, Mummy says she refuses to accept charity. I got so desperate I went through her desk yesterday to see if there was a letter from him. There was and I managed to read some of it before I heard her come in and had to quickly hide it again. He said that money was short at the moment and he had nothing left after he'd paid for our living expenses. He suggested instead of the Holland trip, he would pay my train fare to Scotland and I could spend the Easter holidays with him. He promised to see that I cleaned my teeth, did my revision and went to bed on time. I will be disappointed not to go to Holland but Scotland would be all right too.

April 3rd, 1956.
Cheam. England.

School breaks up tomorrow and Mummy still hasn't said anything about my going to Scotland. I can't mention it because then she'll know I read the letter. It must be more than two years now since I saw my father and he probably thinks I don't want to come. So I wrote a letter to him today and posted it secretly. I explained that I'd love to visit him but that I've got too much school work at present so we'd better wait till the summer holidays after my exams. I hope it reaches him.

May 5th, 1956.
Cheam. England.

Mummy just told me that as soon as exams are over in July we are to go down to Salcombe for the whole summer. She has some friends down there who keep a boat so we will be able to go sailing with them. She's trying to make up to me for the Easter hols disaster, for which I still haven't forgiven her. I don't really like her friends but sailing's something I've always wanted to do and at least it means getting away from here. Ginny's no longer talking to me and has turned several of the other girls against me too. She must have overheard me telling Janet about her father's big bear noises because we were in the library and I realised too late she'd been listening on the other side of the bookshelves. Whoever said schooldays are the best time of your life! This year everything that can has gone wrong and I can't wait for them to end.

*　*　*

Extract from Jake Mullen's diary, 1956.

June 12th 1956.
Nairn. Scotland

Damn that cold-hearted bitch wife of mine to hell! After I read her letter I walked to the top of Crone hill and back before I felt calm enough to read it again and consider my response.

Another year has passed without my seeing my daughter and now she informs me they are to spend the summer in Salcombe with her friend Dinah and her husband. A more meddling, sanctimonious woman than Dinah it would be hard to imagine. She has always fanned the flames of Mary's self-righteousness and done her best to turn the child against me too. The husband, Bill, is too cowardly to stand up for himself and takes the line of least resistance. Such people suck the very goodness out of life and this is the atmosphere in which our child is struggling to grow. Mary will never stop punishing me for the fact that I betrayed her by inflicting upon her the worst insult a man could perpetrate upon his blameless wife - bringing my Jezebel to this country, adulteress, home wrecker and, worst of all, swarthy of skin. She permits no explanation but glories in her martyrdom. In truth she expected nothing less from the pitiful excuse for a man she married.

I have not heard from Beryl since Easter and I begin to wonder if she even receives my letters. There is little I can do except keep on writing in the hope that Mary's conscience will at least prevent her from blocking all communication between us, though as she never ceases to point out, I have forfeited all rights over my child. One day, I pray, when she is old enough to know a bit more of the world and its people, I will be able to explain things to Beryl. I fear she will never understand how deeply losing her grieves my heart.

*   *   *

Notebook entitled 'Lola's Book', written and illustrated with drawings in colourful crayons in 1983 by Jake Mullen's granddaughter, Lola Mullen, aged eight, and found with his papers.

August 8th, 1983.
Nairn, Scotland.

Yesterday Grandpa put up a swing for my birthday in one of the apple trees. I will be eight. The branches of the tree are quite low and when I go really high my feet get mixed up with them. Today I got stuck and hung upside down for a bit then fell down and banged my head. I wasn't hurt but Grandpa made me come in and lie down. Afterwards he wouldn't let me play on the swing so we went to the beach.

It was very hot and there were lots of little blue butterflies in the dunes but on the sands it was too windy. There are shells on the beach and we are collecting them. Grandpa tells me the names and I write them down in my book and draw a picture by each name. So far we have found four kinds, oyster mother of pearl, razor bills, little shiny pink shells which are my favourite and the biggest which are called conch shells. Grandpa says the Greeks used them as musical instruments and you can put them to your ear and hear the sea. Yesterday we found a speckled cowrie, which is quite rare. So far I have paddled but not bathed. The sea is too cold but I hope it will warm up before Mummy comes to fetch me.

Grandpa is helping me with this diary. I ask him about the hard words and he corrects my punctuation. Miss Williams, my teacher, will be very pleased.

This is my favourite place in the whole world.

August 9th.
Nairn, Scotland.

Tomorrow we are to have a surprise visitor. He is a little Indian boy a year younger than me and Grandpa has made me promise to keep his visit a secret between the two of us and not to tell Mummy or Grandma because they disapprove of his family being Indian. When I asked him why he said he'd explain another day. The boy's name is Afzhal and Grandpa says he is quite grown up for his age so he will be a good playmate for me. I am looking forward to it because I have never met an Indian before. Mummy and Grandma don't know any foreigners except at Mummy's work but that's different.

August 10th.
Nairn, Scotland.

Grandpa gave me a tortoise for my birthday. He was in a box at the end of my bed when I woke up. I am calling him Thomas. I took him outside and fed him some lettuce leaves then went in for my breakfast. When I came out again he had disappeared and we found him half way down the lane. It seems tortoises walk quite fast.

The Indian boy arrived just before lunch. He is not black but brown, like a conker but not so red, and he is not a cry baby. We played on the swing then went to the beach. He laughs a lot and likes to play tricks but they are not nasty, more like jokes. One thing I don't like. He calls my grandpa, Grandpa. I think he is just copying me because I am older but when I told him to stop he refused.

August 12th.
Nairn, Scotland.

Today Afzhal and me had a big fight. He was being very annoying and let Thomas out of his box so we had to spend a long time looking for him and almost gave up. When I told him he couldn't go on the swing as a punishment, he got angry and punched me so I grabbed hold of him and pulled his hair, which is quite long, and we fought. Grandpa was very cross. Lola, he said, you are a selfish little girl and at eight years old you should know better. This was unfair and I got very upset. I said it was all Afzhal's fault and he should go home but Grandpa told me to stop being so silly. When Mummy phoned and asked why I was crying I told her Grandpa was cross with me. She said she is coming tomorrow to fetch me. I wish now I hadn't told her but it is too late. When I tried to say sorry to Afzhal he refused to speak to me. Grandpa said that will teach me a lesson. But when he saw how sorry I was, he told me I had a good heart and that he loved me very much.

I will leave this diary here when I go home but will carry on with it next hols.

* * *

Lola Mullen's Diary.

February 24th, 2005.
Isle of Dogs, London.

I've decided to write a diary. I haven't done so since I was a child in Scotland, staying with Grandpa. I wonder what happened to it?

The thing that decided me was sitting on the bus this morning and realising that this year I'll be thirty! Everything's moving so fast. Even the look of this city changes day by day and yet my own life is going nowhere. So, as I passed Paperchase on my way to the office, I went in and bought this notebook and a swish new pen such as I can never resist despite living in the age of the computer. I shall record my thoughts in the attempt to make better sense of my life.

No one admits it but our company, like many others in the square mile, is in deep shit. We overreached ourselves in the euphoria of the election and it looks now like a lot of people will soon be out of a job. Janice, my assistant and a reliable barometer of corporate thinking, is already toadying up to those she considers will be the survivors.

I was standing at my office window, drinking my coffee and psyching myself up for an interview with the boss later that morning, when I noticed a figure down below. He was a point of stillness in the continuous flux of passers-by, criss-crossing the geometric lines of the square. He was staring up at our building and for a moment I had the strange sensation that our gazes met, though this was scarcely possible at a distance of fourteen floors.

I stepped back and in my haste spilt coffee down my skirt and had to go to the ladies to rinse it off. Standing there in my knickers and staring at my reflection in the mirror, I was shocked by my pale face and the dark circles under my eyes. The spiky haircut I've had done makes me look more like a junky than a fashion icon. Must get an early night!

It's evening and I'm back home. Altogether it's been a strange sort of day. This morning as I emerged from the toilet, Janice announced a young man was insisting on seeing me, though he didn't have an appointment. I told her to send him to my office but, if he was still there after ten minutes, to announce I had a client, although that wasn't actually true.

'Quite dishy, if you like small men!' Janice announced.

I watched from my cubicle as he came down the glass-lined corridor in a maze of rippling reflections that reminded me of Omar Sharif's first appearance in the film of 'Lawrence of Arabia'. As soon as he entered my office, I had an uncanny sense that he was the man I'd seen earlier in the square. I also knew I'd seen him before. A couple of nights ago on the bus home from work, he was seated behind me. I'd noticed his reflection in the window because he was staring at me. When I stood up to get off, he seemed about to say something but I ran down the stairs before he could do so.

He gave his name as Afzhal Khan, saying it as if it should mean something to me. Then he looked around him and said,

'Bloody shame!'

'What is?'

'This whole tacky development! What a lost opportunity.'

'Are you an architect?'

'I hope to be one day.'

'D'you mind telling me what you want? I've got another client in a few minutes.'

He smiled, as if he knew it was merely a ruse to get rid of him.

'Your grandfather, Jake Mullen.'

'What about him?'

'He's an old family friend.'

'He died, I'm afraid.'

'I know.'

He paused then added, 'You and I met at his house in Scotland.'

I searched my memory but had no recollection of it.

'When?'

'A long time ago. It was your birthday.'

My mind remained a blank. The next minute Janice put her head round the door to say my client was waiting, though he'd been there less than five minutes.

'Tell him to hang on. I'll be with him shortly,' I snapped.

Azhal got up.

'You're obviously busy. We'll talk another time.'

'Can't you just say what you came for?'

'Don't worry. I'll be in touch.'

And with that he was gone. I was so irritated I almost ran after him and grabbed him at the lift but resisted, not wanting to look like a complete fool. There's something pushy and quite arrogant about him I don't care for.

Feb.27th.

Battersea, London.

I've been at home for three days with a lousy cold and flu-like symptoms. It's as if thick clouds have enveloped me, though outside the weather's a bit more spring-like. There's no food in the house and anyway I can't be bothered to cook. Even my nightly bath is too much effort. I'm wondering if it could be a recurrence of the glandular fever I had two years ago.

I've been thinking about Afzhal Khan and half expected him to have got hold of my home number but no one's called. Except Janice to say she's taking care of things at the office and to stay away as long as I like. No surprise there!

The flat is a tip and I have to do something about it but haven't the energy. The bulbs I carefully planted before Christmas haven't come out because I forgot to water them and Fergus has got so fed up with only dried food, he's taken off. I shall be very sad if he's gone missing.

March 1st.
Battersea, London.

Feeling a bit better, I've spent today writing a letter of resignation to my boss. I've been thinking of making a move for a while now. At least this way he won't have the satisfaction of sacking me, though I'll miss out on any redundancy. Then I phoned my mother to tell her I'm going to Scotland to grandfather's house and to forward any mail. The house is mine through Grandpa's will but the last time I was up there must be almost a year. A woman from the village goes in once a week to keep an eye on things but it's likely to be in a depressing state. I've got stuff of his to sort out and there'll be repairs to see to after two more winters of neglect.

I need to make a decision about selling the place, though since it holds my happiest memories that'll be hard. I might sublet this flat for a while, provided the landlord doesn't get wind of it. Once the panic subsides, there is something oddly exhilarating about no job and no income. And if I feel lonely, I'll get a dog.

Meanwhile the cat's returned.

March 9th.
Train to Inverness.

I'm trying to calm down after the shock of what has just happened, though my writing hand is still shaking.

I arrived at the station and was looking at the departures board, when I became aware of someone standing behind me. I turned round and saw Afzhal Khan.

'This is starting to look like harassment.'

I said it jokingly but he came back quite aggressive.

'You're off to Scotland? I need to speak to you before you go.'

I asked how he knew and he said he'd called my office. Thanks, Janice, I thought.

'There's something of your grandfather's that belongs to me.'

Now I was sure he was bullshitting.

'He kept a diary when he was in India at the end of the Second World War. He promised to give it to me only he died before he could do so.'

'Why would he do that?'

'Your grandfather was very fond of me.'

'I've never heard of any diary. I don't even know who you are.'

He handed me a slip of paper with a telephone number on it.

'If you find it, call that number. I wouldn't want it to get thrown out with the rest of his stuff when you sell up.'

I could hardly believe his cheek.

'Who says I'm selling?'

'Of course, I could always come up and look for myself.'

That was it. I'd had enough.

'This is bullshit! Clear off and leave me alone!'

I walked away. My anger was now mixed with a certain alarm. How come he knew so much about me and Grandpa when I knew nothing about him?

On my way to the platform, I remembered I'd forgotten to arrange for someone to feed Fergus and called my friend Rosheen. I guess I also wanted to tell her about my strange encounter with Afzhal Khan.

When I got into the train, most of the seats were already taken by people lost to the world in their laptops and mobile phones. I found a seat and as the doors were shutting and the whistle blew, I glanced out of the window and there was Afzhal, walking rapidly down the platform checking the carriages as he went. I jumped up and reached the intersection just as he was reopening the door. He gave a nasty grin when he saw me, a look I interpreted as pure animosity. I tried to pull the door shut but he was stronger than me. The train was starting to move and I pushed him with all my might, determined not to let him in. Bracing myself against the frame, I managed to hook one foot around his leg and struggling as if my life depended on it, I jerked him off balance so that he let go his handhold and fell backwards onto the platform just as the door closed and the train began to gather speed. I was shaking and out of breath. I had no idea whether he'd been hurt in his fall and I didn't care. All that mattered was that he was gone. And my fellow passengers hadn't even looked up.

My fear is now that he really will follow me to Scotland.

* * *

Email from Afzhal.Khan@yahoo.com to rmbradford@blueyonder.co.uk. 10.3.05

Hi Nana,

I won't be able to make it to you this weekend. Don't worry. I hurt my back but it's nothing that taking it easy for a while won't put right.

I saw Lola Mullen in her fancy city office. She'd no idea who I was though I recognised her at once. I asked for the diary, which she said she knew nothing about and refused to believe I could have anything to do with 'her' grandfather. No surprise there! I know you said not to upset her but if I have to, I'll go up to Scotland and look for myself. It's our story and we've every right to it.

Best love,
Afzhal

*   *   *

Email to Afzhal.Khan@yahoo.com from rmbradford@blueyonder.co: 11.03.05

Dearest Boy,

What is this problem with your back? You neglect yourself and do too much, what with your job all day and at night working at your art when you should be resting. Take a taxi from the station. I will pay. And let me know in good time when you are coming because I shall be cooking.

I am not surprised to hear about your meeting with Lola. You rush into things and it may well be true that she knows nothing of the diary. It would have been wiser to wait till you got to know her better before demanding it.

In any case you attach too much importance to it. Even if you find it, what will it tell you? You already know who you are. Your identity has never been in question. Nor should your loyalty to a country that gave us shelter be so.

Jake hoped you would be a peacemaker and lay past conflicts to rest. But you seem bent on joining those young hotheads who do their best to resurrect old quarrels, not even of their own making. You would do far better to help build a saner world where difference is tolerated. I may be old but I know how foolish it is to let past conflicts overshadow our lives. What matters, especially for you young ones, is the future.

Take good care of yourself.

Your loving,
Nana

*   *   *

From Lola Mullen's diary.

March 10th. 2005.
Nairn. Scotland.

When the train reached Inverness it was still dark. I found a cab outside the station with the cabbie asleep inside and he agreed to drive me the thirty miles or so along the coast. As we drove east, the day dawned grey and drizzly. The heating in the car wasn't very effective and my jeans and leather jacket weren't much protection against the Scottish cold. The cabbie apologised and offered me a rug. Just being here always makes me feel better.

We stopped off in the village for provisions, which the cabbie insisted on carrying up to the house. He was worried about abandoning me and asked rather sweetly if I wouldn't be lonely. When I assured him I wouldn't, he said his sister lived in the village and wrote down her phone number. I thanked him for everything and when I tried to give him a tip he refused. I feel that nothing bad can befall me here.

Standing as it does behind the dunes, protected by a clump of wind-stunted trees, the house doesn't look too dilapidated. On closer inspection, though, most of the whitewash has worn away, exposing lichen-stained stones and peeling window frames. The garden, once

Grandpa's pride and joy, is now a forlorn wilderness under the wintry sky. I must do something about it.

Inside is equally depressing and bitterly cold. Despite Mrs Tate coming in once a week to light fires, it does little to counteract the damp, unlived-in feel of the place. I pulled back the curtains in the living room and the low winter sun showed up threadbare rugs and a layer of dust over everything. My childhood memories are of a house that was always warm and welcoming, even in the coldest of winters. Its untidiness was part of Grandpa's bohemian attitude to life and a welcome contrast to the sterile order of my grandmother's house.

I've put on all the sweaters I brought, lit a fire, switched on the night storage heaters and set about making the place more cheerful. By the time I'd made up a bed and washed the plates and mugs abandoned in the kitchen sink, it was already dark. I made myself a hot drink and unpacked the food I'd bought, though I didn't feel like cooking. The house is starting to warm up but I've decided to sleep down here tonight, close to the hearth.

March 11th.
Nairn. Scotland.

I slept badly, plagued by a dream that kept returning even after I'd got up from the sofa to make up the fire. Now in the morning light it's hard to recall, except for the atmosphere of menace which I'm unable to shake off. Something was prowling around the house, looking for chinks to prise open, a door or a window. It made no sound and all I could do was wait with baited breath.

At about seven, though it was still dark, I got up and went into the kitchen to make myself a coffee. I started going through the pile of post Mrs Tate has left on the kitchen table, bills mostly and most of those red ones. The bank, it appears, has cancelled my standing orders because I forgot to renew them. Luckily they haven't cut off the electricity yet.

Amongst the bills, I came across a postcard addressed to me and sent shortly after Grandpa's funeral. It shows a picture of Bradford, a handsome area called German town. On the back in minute, almost illegible handwriting it says, 'Dear Miss Mullen, Please get in touch at your earliest convenience' and is signed R. Mazrak. In the top right hand corner there's an address. I've been trying to think if I know anyone in Bradford or ever heard of anyone called Mazrak. No one, except my mother and Rosheen, knows this address or that I'm here. Except, of course, Afzhal Khan!

Feeling better after eating I began a systematic search of the house, looking for this mysterious diary. If it exists it must be here somewhere, otherwise Grandma or Mother would have destroyed it long ago, as they did all Grandpa's other belongings. I admit I'm curious since I know nothing of his early life or his war-time experiences. All I remember is Grandma saying he returned from the war a changed man, and I knew she meant something she couldn't bring herself to speak about. It was part of the general atmosphere of blame she sent out whenever he was mentioned, like a poisonous fog. My mother had grown up with it but even as a child I felt the need to distance myself from it. Whenever I asked my mother if she knew what had happened between her parents, she claimed not to. Talking, she said, only upset my grandmother so she'd never asked.

The most likely place for the diary is Grandpa's desk but a thorough search has turned up only an old photo album from one of the drawers. This, however, contains surprises of its own. Most of the photos are of people I don't know, long dead judging by their clothes. But there are also some of myself as a child and one of a small dark-skinned boy. He is dressed like a miniature maharaja, in a turban and an embroidered coat with a toy sword strapped to his side. I studied the picture closely and to my profound disturbance I have concluded that the child might well be Afzhal Khan.

And that's not all. On the following page there is a photo of myself aged around eight with the same little Indian boy, standing in the garden under the apple tree next to the swing. We are facing one another, heads thrown back and laughing with the unrestrained merriment of childhood. How come I have no recollection of this or any other meeting?

In a desperate search for some memory, I've been racking my brains and have at last managed to come up with something. A boy, who must be Afzhal, and I are playing in the garden and he keeps calling my Grandpa 'Grandpa'. I am furious with him because I know he's only doing it to annoy me, but he refuses to stop. How could I have wiped all this?

March 12th.
Nairn. Scotland.

I've been digging around in my memory and other things are starting to resurface. For my eighth birthday, Grandpa announced a surprise. A little Indian boy is coming to stay but it's to be a secret between us and I mustn't tell Mummy or Grandma. I'm not sure about this. Scotland has always been my place, mine and Grandpa's.

Feeling somewhat paranoid, as it grew dark I began hearing noises outside the house and became convinced there was someone there. I put on a coat, armed myself with a stout stick and went out, only to be confronted by a huge stag standing in the flower bed, happily munching some hardy berries left over from autumn. When he saw me he calmly finished his mouthful, turned away and ambled off into the gloaming.

However, the threat of Afzhal showing up remains. I can't get out of my mind his evil expression as we struggled in the doorway of the train. I wonder should I call the taxi man's sister?

March 13th.
Nairn. Scotland.

I've survived another night and not only that, I've found the diary! I started my search again as soon as it got light, going through every room and cupboard until in desperation I returned to the desk. Foraging around at the back of one of the drawers, my fingers closed over a small handle, which I swear had not been there before. I pulled it and the rear panel slid to one side, exposing a hidden compartment. I felt around and brought out a battered leather-bound notebook together with some papers and exercise books. On the inside page of the diary was stamped the name of Grandpa's regiment and underneath in handwriting, 'This book is the property of Major Jake Mullen, Wana Brigade, Waziristan.'

I've spent most of the day reading it and when I came to the end, I fell asleep in the chair. Tonight I've decided to get a proper night's sleep in a real bed.

March 14th.
Nairn. Scotland.

I awoke to a glorious, crisp morning, feeling as if a weight has been lifted from me. The diary brings Grandpa vividly to life. I imagine I hear his voice as he describes those strange events that took place so long ago and far away. It's almost as if he's with me again. But the question remains, what is Afzhal Khan's relationship to this story? And if what he says is true, why did Grandpa promise the diary to him?

I read it through a second time then made coffee, put on Grandpa's old duffle coat, which is still hanging on the peg by the back door, and went into the garden for some air. No stag today but the first of the daffodils and some little blue scillas - signs of spring at last. I found a spade and did some digging in the vegetable patch, mostly for the exercise since I've no seeds to sow. The earth was hard and frosty and from time to time the wind blew the clouds away and the sky cleared, leaving those shreds we call mares' tails in a washed, blue heaven. And wherever I am, I can smell the sea.

Later I walked into the village for some milk, eggs and bread but didn't hang around in case Afzhal shows up and tries to break in. It occurred to me he might even have a key! I've been asking myself how he was so certain of the diary's existence when I knew nothing about it. The answer has to be that Grandpa told him about it and that makes me feel bad. It's a bit like finding out your lover's been unfaithful.

It puts in question my whole idea of the relationship I had with Grandpa and I realise now how jealous of Afzhal I must have been from the moment he appeared in our lives. Perhaps that's the reason I've blocked out his existence. Most school holidays my mother delivered me to Scotland and left. Grandpa and I used to drive to Edinburgh, Glasgow or the islands in his old Ford car. Once we took the ferry to Ireland and spent a couple of nights in a bed and breakfast place where he knew the landlady. I loved travelling with him, all the stories he told about the places we visited, talking non stop about local history and the people he'd met on his journeys - a world away from the deathly hush of my grandmother's house. But I don't recall him ever mentioning the war or India.

March 15th.
Nairn. Scotland

Reading through his diary for a third time, I was suddenly struck by the name Mazrak and went in search of the postcard from Bradford. I fished it out of the waste bin in the kitchen and found a magnifying glass in a pot with some dried out biros on Grandpa's desk. I carefully examined the signature and there can be little doubt. The name is the same as the one in the diary. Can this be a coincidence or is there a connection between whoever sent that card and a bandit in Waziristan sixty-odd years ago? It hardly seems credible.

March 16th.
Train – Inverness to Bradford

I've decided the only way to solve this mystery is to go to Bradford and find whoever sent the postcard. Also the water heater's broken down and I've had enough of boiling up kettles. Before I left I found the old tin bath and had a good scrub down in front of the fire like in the old days. I was beginning to smell.

I've continued to have some weird dreams. Last night it was the little black prince from the photo. He was seated on a throne in a great hall. His feet didn't touch the ground but stuck straight out in front of him and at first I thought he was a dwarf or some sort of clockwork toy. But as I approached he leapt down and began to swell until his silk clothes burst from his body like an old snake skin. With one hand he wrenched the turban from his head so that his sleek black hair flowed down over his shoulders and with the other he pulled his sword from its scabbard and brandished it over me. He was now so big he almost filled the room and started moving around with a peculiar writhing gait, grimacing like the samurai in a Kurosawa film. I could feel his hot breath on my face and tried to run, but I couldn't move. Then I woke. Strangely this dream is not as disturbing as the previous night's.

I have no idea what I shall find in Bradford or why the mysterious R.Mazrak has summoned me but I shall no doubt find out.

*　*　*

Afzhal.Khan@yahoo.com to rmbradford@blueyonder.co.uk: March 16th

Hi Nana,

Great news! You remember that competition I entered for a sculpture to commemorate the cricket match between the visiting team from Pakistan and the people of Bradford? Out of hundreds, my design has been chosen! It's to be cast in bronze and there'll be a grand unveiling in the New Year. I'm coming up to see a representative from the Arts Committee and will call you as soon as I get the date.

By the way, any news from Lola? I'll give her a couple more days then I'm going to Scotland.

You'll see, you'll be proud of me yet!

Love as always,
Afzhal

*　*　*

From Lola Mullen's diary. March 17th. 2005. Bradford.

I arrived in Bradford late this afternoon and now that I'm here, I wonder what I'm doing. Though I have to find out who is this Mazrak person and what he wants, at the same time the thought of rooting up the past makes me uneasy.

I've taken a room in the Railway Hotel. It's an old-fashioned place, hardly changed by the looks of it since the 1950s with wide staircases and high ornate ceilings. My bedroom is like something out of a Hammer horror Dracula movie - huge mahogany bed with matching wardrobe and red damask curtains tied back with thick gold braid. It has a view across the railway lines and the lights of the city are very pretty. I'm going out now for a curry in one of Bradford's famed Indian restaurants. Tomorrow I shall decide what to do.

March 18th.
Bradford.

Last night I tossed and turned for hours, the fault no doubt of the curry, and finally fell asleep as the birds began to sing. When I made it down to breakfast they were clearing it away but with amazing good humour offered to cook me eggs and bacon. I opted for a cup of coffee and half a grapefruit.

I showed the address on the postcard to the hotel manageress, who gave me instructions about which bus to take for a neighbourhood she referred to without irony as Little Bombay. In outward appearance it looks like any other suburb only the streets are a bit cleaner and the corner shops display a better range of fruit and veg. I got off the bus and checked the number of the house, which I had tattooed on my hand.

No one answered the door and I was standing on the doorstep wondering what to do next when I noticed an old man gesticulating wildly in the window of the neighbouring house. I thought he might be in some sort of trouble so hopped over the dividing wall. But when he finally managed to get the window open, he barely had time to hiss 'She's out!', when a woman wearing a sari under her cardigan rushed in, shoved him aside and slammed the window shut. I turned to go but the front door opened and the same woman called me from the step, demanding to know what I wanted. I replied politely that I was looking for someone called Mazrak and she said Mrs Mazrak was out at present and enquired whether I was from Social Services. When I said no, she went on to explain that Mrs Mazrak lived alone with no family of her own to care for her so had to go to the Day Centre each day for her dinner. She left me in no doubt that this situation was a result of her own failing more than any misfortune. I asked for directions to the Day Centre and set off. So R.Mazrak turns out to be a woman!

I got off the bus outside a depressing-looking sixties building. Inside there was an attempt to make the place cheerful with children's paintings and posters advertising coming events for Easter pinned onto magnolia shaded walls. About fifty old people were seated at tables eating dinner and what struck me was the noise - a high-pitched chatter like birds in an aviary, quite unlike the church-like hush of Grandma's social gatherings. I grabbed one of the helpers, identified by her overall and hairnet, and asked if she could point out Mrs Mazrak. She directed me to the far side of the room.

Three people were seated at a formica-topped table. The first was a heavily built woman, who sat without moving or speaking and stared unseeingly into her lap. The second was a tiny, bird-like woman with a wrinkled brown face and black eyes like a robin constantly on the alert. She wore a grey cardigan much too big for her over blue silk trousers and her hair was pulled back into a neat plait. The third occupant was a man wearing a sea captain's cap, fisherman's sweater and canvas trousers. He stood up and gallantly offered me a seat.

'Captain Billy Mather, at your service! And your name, lovely lady?'

I told him Lola and he went off into a riff about Dolores, the Lady of the Sorrows and hoped that didn't apply to me.

'What brings you here to Oz?' he demanded.

It turned out he meant not Australia but Oz as in Wizard of, an apt description for such a zany place. It was impossible to get a word in edgeways and I was becoming increasingly irritated, when bingo was announced and a volunteer came round with cards and pencils.

'Likes a flutter does Madam M.,' Billy said, nodding towards the tiny Indian woman at his side.

She took the pencil from the big woman seated on her left and gently turned it over so that the lead end rested on the card then closed her fingers over it. I decided to intervene before the game started.

'Mrs Mazrak, I'm Lola Mullen. You sent me a postcard.'

She turned her bright robin's gaze on me.

'You know my grandson, I believe. Afzhal Khan.'

'He's your grandson? Yes. I've met him.'

'Ah! Our Lady of the Sorrows comes seeking that handsome young relative of yours. Take pity on her, Madam M.!' the old man interrupted.

'You're an old fool, Billy Mather,' she snapped and turned back to me. 'The game is starting. I can't talk to you now. Come to my house at 6.30. I go to bed at eight so don't be late.'

Her tone was so abrupt I almost decided to take the train back to London at once. Instead I killed the intervening hours at the cinema, where I fell asleep and ended up being late.

When I arrived she answered the door, saying crossly,

'You have no manners and no sense of time!'

I've rarely met anyone so rude or able to put one's back up so fast. Nevertheless, I followed her down the hall to the kitchen, which was immaculately clean and tidy and looked as though very little cooking actually took place there. She made tea in a china pot and offered me a biscuit, which was soggy and well past its sell by date. Unlike most Indian women I know of, food obviously isn't her thing.

'Your grandfather was a true English gentleman. Not that that seems to have rubbed off on the rest of his family!' she declared.

If she was deliberately trying to provoke me, I was determined to stay calm.

'As a Scot he wouldn't have been flattered. How did you meet him?'

'In India.'

There was a pause before she added,

'My name is Raza. If you've read his diary, you should know who I am.'

I stared at her in astonishment.

'Raza, the bandit's daughter?'

'You find that hard to believe?'

'Impossible. All that's so long ago and far away.'

I did a quick calculation in my head. It was just possible if this woman was even older than she looked.

'I am an old woman who has outlived her time. This city is full of such people.'

'Did Grandpa bring you back to England with him? Was that why he left my grandmother?'

She gave a short laugh, a sort of bark, and I saw the mockery in her robin's eyes.

'It seems that like the rest of your family you do not understand the desire of a man to be a knight in shining armour. It far outweighs desire for love!'

'I don't understand.'

'Are you interested in the truth?'

'It's what I'm here for.'

She looked at me as if trying to gauge my sincerity.

'Jake offered me safety and shelter in England. When your grandmother found out, she assumed like you that he had fallen in love with me. I don't blame her. They'd scarcely seen one another for four years and were almost strangers. But mostly it was my race, not her husband's feelings for another woman, she found unbearable. She forbade him ever to contact her again. For years he sent her money but he wasn't allowed to see his child.'

'And your child?'

'He gave us a name and a home. His wife being Catholic would never divorce him.'

'Did you love him?'

'I respected him and I was grateful.'

How lukewarm that sounded! For her sake Jake had lost everything - home, wife and child. And yet this woman expressed no love for him. Her eyes were hard as pebbles in her wrinkled brown face and showed neither warmth nor regret.

And then I thought of Afzhal. If this is true, it seems we do share a grandfather after all!

March 19th.
Bradford, England.

Last night the fearsome warrior of my dream appeared again and this time I could not mistake that I was the object of his fury. His eyes oozed tears of blood, which trickled down his cheeks into the hairs at the corners of his mouth, bright red drops clinging to the black hairs of his beard as he raised his sword and circled it above his head. But instead of thrusting it into me he began to turn, slowly at first then faster and faster. Round and round he went, drumming his feet on the ground and uttering short war-like cries, until finally he dissolved like a spinning-top into a blur of movement.

I woke up and went to the bathroom. I looked as if I'd done ten rounds with Mohammed Ali and realised I'd once more missed breakfast. I avoided the dining room and went down the road for a cup of tea and a slice of toast in a local caff, more suited to my mood. Back at the hotel the manageress called me over and handed me a note. It was from Raza Mazrak with an address in the city where she said I would find Afzhal. Despite having decided to take the train back to London, the rational part of me knows I must go there and confront him. I will have no peace till I sort this out.

So I took the bus to the Rothermere Estate as directed. As we passed row upon monotonous row of dreary houses, a feeling of desolation came over me at the soullessness of the place. It reflected a dreariness inside me too and I felt a tide of grief swelling like a dam that might burst at any minute. I longed for some all-consuming fire to engulf the whole landscape and me with it. Perhaps then, like the Phoenix, something fresh and new might rise up from the ashes.

The bus driver announced the end of the line and I had a moment of panic, trying to remember what I was doing there. I stayed in my seat until everyone else had got off the bus and he asked if I was all right. I didn't feel all right but I remembered I was looking for the old steel mill and asked if he could direct me. He pointed up the road to a big shed, set back on a patch of waste ground a short distance away. I thanked him and started walking. The other passengers had disappeared into the estate behind us but when I glanced back he was still standing there, watching me. I had the queer feeling that he and I were the last two people on earth.

As I came level with the hangar, I saw through its open doors sparks flying from the great maw of the furnace. Masked figures toiled in the gloom and it was like some apocalyptic vision of hell. So I walked rapidly on, not stopping till I came to the grassy hill that overlooked the city. From the scattering of litter, it appeared to be a favoured spot with picnickers.

Far below, the motorway with its matchbox cars snaked around the skyscrapers. I had a vision of all the millions of souls that had gathered here from all corners of the earth, wave upon wave of migrants like the Children of Israel in Grandpa's diary. When the Second World War ended and the empire finally imploded, its soldiers came here looking for their reward for fighting a cause they didn't understand and was not their own. Instead, they found themselves stranded amongst strangers, who knew nothing of their history or even recognised a common fate.

'Nice, isn't it!'

I turned to see a pasty-faced girl no more than seventeen with a toddler in a pushchair, seated on the grass.

'Lovely,' I said indifferently. I was in no mood for conversation.

'I come here whenever the weather's fine,' the girl persisted. 'My brother does scrap down at the mill. Most days I bring him his dinner.'

She indicated a sandwich box sticking out of a plastic bag stuffed with packets of crisps and baby stuff. The baby made crowing noises and reached out its grubby hands.

'Little monkey!' she said tenderly and burst open a bag of crisps.

She gave some to the baby, who crushed them in its tiny fist trying to stuff them into its mouth.

'Want some?'

I shook my head. All I could think of in my wretched mood was how breeding these dysfunctional families is one of the few things we Brits are good at.

'You're not from round here, are you?'

'No. London.'

'I've never been.' She sounded wistful. 'Perhaps in a year or two when this one's a bit older.'

'How old is she?' I asked, in an effort to be friendly.

'Fourteen months. She already says a few words. Dog, biccit and kiss.'

The girl pursed her lips and screwed up her eyes as she kissed the air. The child imitated her in a paroxysm of delight and for a moment their faces reminded me of my dream warrior.

'I don't know much about babies,' I said.

'Me neither, till I had her. Mum always said you learn on the job. She died last year.'

'I'm sorry.'

'At least they let us keep the flat. I'm starting college in a couple of weeks.'

'That's great.'

'Yes. I'm looking forward to it. Can't live off scrap the rest of me days!'

Such faith in the ultimate goodness of life must surely be God-given. For me it's impossible, a thought I find both depressing and humbling.

As we descended the hill together the girl pointed out her brother, chatting with a group of men from the hangar taking a cigarette break. She made her way towards them and her brother took off his visor to greet her. With his shaved head and prematurely lined face, he looked nothing like her but when he bent down to greet the baby, I could see more of a resemblance.

As I turned away, I saw Afzhal coming towards me. His hair was pulled back into a ponytail and his face camouflaged by dirt but his slightly strutting walk was unmistakable.

'What d'you do in this place?' I asked, for something to say.

'Smelting and welding for my sculpture. Did you find the diary?'

'If that's all you wanted, why not just call me?'

'It's easier to see face to face if you're lying. Have you brought it?'

His insulting manner seemed calculated to provoke but I refused to rise.

'So you did find it.'

Still I did not reply. He turned away and started walking towards the hill. I couldn't let it go at that so I followed him.

When I reached the top, he'd lain down on the damp grass. Despite the chill of the fading afternoon, the air was fresh up there, compared to the fumes from the furnace. A mist was gathering over the city but on the hill it was still bright. Stretched out on the ground and bathed in the sun's last rays, he looked like some bronze effigy. I squatted down a few feet away. His eyes were closed and he was so still that after a few minutes I nudged him, worried that he'd stopped breathing. He turned his head and grinned at me. It wasn't a friendly grin and for some reason I felt tears welling up inside me.

'You frightened me. You weren't moving.'

He pulled himself up on his elbows and regarded me in silence, until I looked away.

'Tell you what,' he said. 'I'll make you a deal.'

'If it's money, I don't have any.'

'It's not money. You give me the diary and I'll tell you what I know about our family history.'

He made an odd barking sound, reminiscent of Raza.

'I forgot! According to you we don't have one.'

I raised my eyes to his.

'Raza had a child with Jake, didn't she?'

'Ask her.'

'Why should she tell me the truth?'

'She's the most truthful person I know. Unlike your family, who've wiped our existence.'

'I just discovered your existence.'

He considered this for a moment, then said, 'Raza lost the child she was expecting on the journey to England. Not that it made any difference to Jake, who kept his promise to care for her as if she were his own.'

'And then they had a child of their own? Your mother?'

He nodded.

'Were they together long?'

'No, but they remained friends.'

'And your father?'

'He was from Kashmir. My parents were killed there in an ambush when I was four. Raza brought me up.'

He sat up, brushing the dead grass from his hands.

'Anything else you want to know?'

'Jake must have been very much in love with Raza.'

He looked at me pityingly and said, 'You don't understand anything, do you? Abdul was the love of his life.'

On the bus back to the city, my mind went over the tangled web that is our family history. For three generations, in the name of family pride, people have done their best to conceal illicit love and mixed race offspring. Today such things are commonplace. But sixty years ago people considered them shameful, secrets to be kept close. Though attitudes have changed, the jealousy and bitterness go on spreading their poison from one generation to the next, despite almost no one being able to recall what started it. Does what I now know free me? I'm not sure. Perhaps it's too soon to tell. What I mostly feel is regret, for all the foolishness that has left me bereft.

March 20th.
Bradford

I decided, before I leave, to make one more call on Raza. By the time I reached her house, it was almost dark and I was afraid she'd refuse to answer the door. When eventually she did, I held out the diary wrapped in brown paper. It was the real thing, not the copy I'd had made. I figured I owed her that much. She looked at it and for a moment her hand hovered over the battered leather cover, as if caressing it. Then she said,

'Come with me. I too have something to show you.'

I followed her upstairs to a bedroom that overlooked the garden. Inside, a roof and walls had been constructed of brightly coloured cloth, with rugs and cushions spread out over the floor in the manner of a Bedouin's tent. Two leather chests stood against one cloth wall, which Raza said were called yakdarns from the yaks who transported them. Out of one she pulled a pile of neatly folded garments and laid them out on the divan. She selected a tunic made of silk and richly embroidered. She held it up against me to check the size. Then she began searching for a pair of trousers to go with it, discarding several until she'd found what she wanted. Lastly she brought out a curved sword encased in a purple velvet scabbard with an embossed silver handle.

'Put these on,' she commanded.

I took off my jeans and jacket and stood there in teeshirt and pants, whilst she looked me up and down.

'What a skinny thing you are! Still, like me the men won't desire you any the less.'

I put on the clothes and she handed me a pair of tall calf boots to go with them. They were a bit big but OK with a pair of thick socks. She led me to the long mirror to observe the effect.

'What a handsome young warrior you make!'

She opened a drawer in one of the smaller chests, brought out a kohl pencil and began darkening my eyebrows. Then she drew a dashing moustache on my upper lip and when she had finished, stood back to survey her handiwork. I raised my sword at my reflection in the glass and took up a warlike stance. She clapped her hands in delight.

'Very good! Now let's see what those Khumals next door have to say when they see you. They'll get the shock of their lives!'

A full moon illuminated the garden as it climbed over the horizon like a great yellow cheese. Stepping out onto the grass, I was suddenly filled with boundless energy. I raised my sword high in the air and tried out a couple of feints in the direction of the neighbour house.

Raza clapped her hands in delight.

'Very good! I can see their scared rabbit faces pressed against the window.'

I sliced my way across the lawn in a series of leaps and bounds. Moonlight glinted off my sword as I chopped and pounced and twirled. And then, out of sheer exuberance, I began to whirl. I could feel every stone and worm cast through the thin soles of my calf boots but I spun faster and faster. The silken ends of my embroidered tunic fanned out around me like the skirts of a whirling dervish and one by one my cares slipped from me like baggage from a packhorse, as I spun like a top.

I lost all sense of time but, at length, whatever mechanism drove me began to wind down. I ran out of steam, lost my balance and hurtled off in the direction of the bushes. My sword flew from my hand and as I grabbed the air for something to break my fall, someone seized hold of me and held me fast. I clung on, head spinning, and when at length I opened my eyes I was looking into the face of Afzhal. Cautiously he released me but when I tottered, he caught me again till I regained my balance.

'Where did you get those clothes?' he said, when I had regained my breath.

'Raza. Do they belong to you?'

He shook his head.

'They're her father's, I believe.'

'Mazrak, the bandit? No wonder I feel so powerful!'

Raza emerged out of the darkness, her eyes bright with merriment.

'What d'you think, Afzhal?' she said. 'She makes a fine warrior, doesn't she!'

Her laughter rippled into the night.

* * *

Email from Afzhal.Khan@yahoo.com to rmbradford@blueyonder,co,uk: Dec.30th 2005

Dearest Nana,

The sculpture unveiling is to be on Jan 10th. By all means invite Lola. I was going to call her anyway but couldn't come up with a good excuse. I hear you laugh. But perhaps you don't recall how fearsome she is when she feels herself slighted.

We could all have dinner afterwards in the posh hotel where they're putting me up, all expenses paid.

And don't forget. Gladrags will be worn!

All love,

Afzhal

* * *

lolamullen@hotmail.com to Afzhal.Khan@yahoo.com: Dec.31st, 2005

Hi Afzhal,

What an auspicious omen for the start of a New Year! I received the invitation to your grand sculpture opening from Raza and shall be honoured to attend. I understand the sculpture is to be called 'Phoenix', something new and splendid rising from the ashes of the past. Just what's needed at a time like this.

On the subject of changes, I've made a few myself since returning to London. I am now the proud renter of a semi-basement in Queen's Park, with a small south-facing garden and a rising enthusiasm for growing things. I also have a temporary job, covering for someone on maternity leave at the local bookshop. It doesn't pay much but I get to read the books.

I've decided to sell the house in Scotland so if you wish to go there and see if there's anything you want, I can arrange for you to have a key. It's not been an easy decision and for a while I thought about living there. But I realised that was impractical since I couldn't afford to maintain it and have accepted the inevitable. It's time to stop hanging onto the past and to move on!

I've also thought a lot more about our meeting all those years ago and a few more memories have resurfaced. Like persuading you to climb the hollow tree and you getting stuck, for which I got the blame. Then when Grandpa caught us eating the candied fruits he'd been saving for Christmas, you claimed it was your idea and you took the blame.

You may not realise it but you were the only playmate I had as a child. Before I met you and Raza I used to fantasise about having another family, my real family. Now it seems it wasn't just a dream! Perhaps I believed it because Grandpa talked of you even before he brought about our meeting. Who knows what rapprochement he might have brought about, had he been just a little braver. I know that's easy for me to say but if we'd been able to talk openly and honestly, we might not have wasted so much time.

What I want above all is to put an end to the amnesia and make sure that what's been unearthed is never buried again. So I've decided to write down our family saga, or as much of it as I can piece together. Perhaps we could make it a joint effort, with the help of Raza?

Meanwhile I look forward very much to our next meeting and to celebrating your big occasion.

Affectionately yours,
Lola